f
wol

Wolff, Miles

Season of the owl

DATE		
FEB 1 1 1981	AUG 1 1990	
MAR 4 1981		
MAR 2 5 1981		
APR 1 5 1981		
MAY 2 7 1981		
JUN 3 1981		
JUL 8 1981		
AUG 1 2 1981		
OCT 7 1981		
APR 1 3 1988		

SEASON
OF
THE
OWL

Also by Miles Wolff
How It All Began

SEASON OF THE OWL

Miles Wolff

STEIN AND DAY/*Publishers*/New York

First published in 1980
Copyright © 1980 by Miles Wolff
All rights reserved
Designed by Louis A. Ditizio
Printed in the United States of America
Stein and Day/*Publishers*/Scarborough House
Briarcliff Manor, N.Y. 10510

1981

Library of Congress Cataloging in Publication Data

Wolff, Miles.
    Season of the owl.

    I. Title.
PZ4.W85694Se   [PS3573.0536]   813'.54   80-51607
ISBN 0-8128-2744-9

To Ann and Lila

SEASON
OF
THE
OWL

1

You think, perhaps, you will turn off and drive through the town. There is no reason, but you have a little time and it would be good to see how it has grown. You take an exit off the interstate that wasn't even built then. Congress had just authorized President Eisenhower to spend the money, to build a network of roads for a national defense highway. There will be changes, for it is said to be one of the progressive cities of the southeast. It is never "South" with a capital anymore, for that was a state of mind. It is now southeast, and industries and people are flocking to its borders. Progress is what matters, and as you drive, it could be almost any city in the country with the new malls, shopping centers, and developments.

But it is not any city. It is somewhere you left many years before. It doesn't seem that long ago, and you don't feel that *much older, but it has been long. It will be good to see the town, to remember some of the old places. It was a good time, a pleasant period of life, when growing up seemed the only thing you were ever destined to do. Being an adult never entered your mind. What year was it, that last Christmas? It must have been 1957, and it would have been nice for time to have stood still so that the only thing you need worry about was getting a Christmas tree.*

N OW, why did Will put up such an awful looking tree every year? It's hard to account for some people's taste, but I was on top of the roof in the wind and blowing snow trying to hold the tree steady. Will, himself, was trying to tie it firm to the chicken wire for support so he could start putting on the outdoor lights. Of course, I tried to tell Will how bad the tree looked, but he never listened. I couldn't get over how a grown man could get so excited about Christmas, or maybe not so much Christmas as putting that awful looking tree on the roof. He was late this year, and with only four days left until Christmas and me just out for my Christmas break, he'd woken up early on Saturday and told me it was time to go cut down the tree.

You could never tell about Will. Given the choice between picking the right time to do something and the wrong time, Will, often as not, would pick the wrong time. And why he'd pick this morning to go cut down a tree I didn't know, but as I looked out the window I sure knew it was the wrong time. It was beginning to snow, and it was going to be cold and wet, and most likely Will's old Studebaker would get stuck in the mud, and then I'd have to push it.

Will put some lumpy oatmeal in front of me, and as I ate it and read the sports pages, I began to think about the snow. I sure hoped it wouldn't stick, and I saw it was still melting on the streets. Not that I didn't like snow. Far from it. It usually was the best thing that could happen. But it was just the wrong time for it to snow. We usually had two or three snows a year at most, and they'd come in January or February when school was in session. The good thing about the school board was that snow really scared them, and if five or six inches fell, we'd have a day off. The year before it had snowed six inches, and we'd had a week of

13

no school. The board said they were worried about those big orange school buses slipping on the roads. School boards tended to worry about funny things. But with this snow, if it stuck it would use up one of the snows, and there was no school to let out.

"Hey, Will. Did you see where Pete Brennan scored 27 last night?" I was still reading the paper, yelling out to Will who was washing the dishes. Carolina had won again. "That makes 37 straight. I don't think they'll ever lose." Will mumbled something, mainly because he wasn't a basketball fan, but then I wasn't really telling him because I thought he should be educated. I was pushing for a basketball for Christmas, and I wanted to make certain. A few well-placed hints couldn't hurt. Pete Brennan was my basketball hero, and I was determined to be like him, although I was a little unclear how you could grow to make yourself 6′8″. Still, I needed a basketball to start.

I turned to the movie page to see what was playing, but nothing good was on at the show. I couldn't believe that they'd held Pat Boone in "April Love" over for the second week. How could anybody with good sense go to see that, except a bunch of silly girls who obviously didn't have good sense? "Around the World in Eighty Days" was starting Christmas day at the Avon, and I'd have to go see that except they were charging $1.50 for matinees and $2.00 at night. I sure hoped some relatives would send money for Christmas instead of socks.

Will was rushing me through my oatmeal, telling me to hurry up, and you'd have thought it was a school day the way he was rushing. That tree wasn't going anywhere while I ate my oatmeal and read the paper. But Will was set on hurrying out, and I didn't even have a chance to check all the scores before he had me go down to the cellar and get the rope and gloves and saw. I'm not sure "cellar" was the correct word, I'd sure seen better cellars, but because it was under the first floor and a little in the ground Will called it a cellar.

I went around to the back of the house and slid open the slip latch and took two steps down. "Damn!" I hit my head on the ceiling, and I sure hoped Will hadn't heard me. He didn't really take with my cussing, although I'd heard him say worse when he was really mad. I rubbed my head, thinking how dumb I was. I'd grown a couple of inches over the fall and kept forgetting and bumping my head.

As I carried the saw and rope out of the cellar I felt like cussing again. The snow was started to stick. It just wasn't time. Will, however, was delighted and couldn't understand my lack of good humor. "Tom, boy, we may have a white Christmas if this stuff sticks. Why, do you know it's been twenty years since we've had a white Christmas in this part of the state?" Will could really make me sick when he talked like that. If I was getting a basketball for Christmas, assuming Will was smart enough to figure out my hints, how could I go down to the playground and shoot the basketball if snow was on the ground? Besides, snow should wait until January so I could miss school.

I was really surprised, but the old Studebaker started on the first crank, and we took off with black smoke pouring out of the exhaust. Will was unbelievable, and he was going on about how everyone in Centerville liked the tree. He said seven people had called the day before to find out when the tree was going up. I couldn't believe anyone would call for that miserable tree. Will kept up his chatter as we passed over the railroad tracks and then out past the textile mill. Huge clouds of white smoke were coming out of the smokestack of the mill, and I could see the workers inside the old building doing whatever it took to make the denim that was used in those bib overalls the farmers wore to town on Saturdays.

Our trip would take maybe twenty minutes, and it was over the old back road that eventually ended up in Denton. I'd never been to Denton, but all the guys in school joked about how Denton had the biggest hicks in the world. I guessed I didn't want to go to Denton. We were out toward the country when Will started talking about how much that area had grown up. It was true that some mobile homes had been put up, and a few, small, red-brick houses were beginning to dot the farmland we

15

passed. But it was still pretty rural, and I sure wouldn't have called it part of the city like Will did. But Centerville was growing, and a couple of new industries had moved to the town in the last few years. Mill workers were getting paid a little more now, and they no longer had to live in the mill village. The land we passed was the red clay that wasn't good for growing much of anything, so I figured most of the people who had moved out here still worked in town.

Even with my bad mood about being woken up early and the snow and all, I still sort of enjoyed the ride with Will. He always talked a lot on these trips, and by the time we got to the farm his excitement over the tree had rubbed off on me. We pulled off the road to an old frame house, and Will got out and went and knocked on the front door. I was busy opening the trunk and getting out the saw when an older woman dressed in an apron with a dish towel in her hand came to the door. "Why, Will, I've been lookin' for you. And is that little Tommy out there? My, my, how he's growing. Shootin' up like a weed. Tooom-mmmmmeee! . . ." she yelled out, and I waved over to her. I stood by the car as Will talked a few seconds, and as he came back to the car the woman yelled out again. "Now, you men, pick out a good tree this year, you hear." We smiled and started walking over a wet, plowed field to the woods.

Pick out a good tree, I thought. That would be next to impossible. I used to wonder how the other trees looked so good and Will's looked so bad. One day I wandered down to a tree lot by the American Legion hut. They were selling all those beautifully formed spruces and the like, and I asked the man where he got them. He had on his funny American Legion hat and told me they were shipped from Canada. Now, you'd have thought Will could have spent four or five bucks and helped out the American Legion and bought a decent tree in the bargain. But oh no, he had to go out to the country each year and cut one down, and the only thing this section of the state had were those awful looking cedars. Even then Will couldn't pick out a half decent tree. He always picked one that was way too big. ("They've got to be able

16

to see it from the road, Tom,") and it was usually lopsided and then we'd have to tie it down on the roof and go through all that mess. But there certainly wasn't any arguing with Will when he came to get his Christmas tree, and I just went along with whatever he wanted. Some of the guys at school would make comments, but I could take an ugly tree if that's what Will wanted.

"Tom, I think I see a good one. See down there at the bottom of the hill. Hurry up. Let's check it out." I peered down to where Will was pointing and saw what was undoubtedly the worst tree I had ever seen. Even from a distance I could tell it had a double trunk and would never do, but Will was now four strides ahead of me, and it was all I could do to keep up. The snow had melted in the red clay of the plowed field, and I was wearing Will's old galoshes. They were about two sizes too big for me, and every time I took a step, the mud would suck them in. A couple of times I almost pulled my shoes off trying to keep up with Will as the red mud sucked me back.

He was already sizing up the tree when I reached it, and he turned to me. "She's a beauty, don't you think?" I pointed out the double trunk which he hadn't noticed. "You know, Tom, you may be right. Let's look around a bit more, and if we can't find one we'll come back for this one."

Now came the part I hated, for we would start searching through the brambles and underbrush—for some reason the cedars grew in that mess—and I would always get scratched two or three times as the stickers and briars pushed through my jeans. Will was still going a mile a minute from tree to tree until I heard him call from a hollow down by a little creek. "Here it is, Tom. Bring the saw." I followed his voice to where he stood beside a tree that was over ten feet tall.

"Don't you think it's a little big?" I asked, but Will was convinced it was perfect, and at least the shape resembled a Christmas tree. I kneeled at the trunk and started sawing as Will pulled on the tree to give me an angle. In a few minutes my arm got tired and Will took over.

17

When the sawing was finished, Will had me hold it at ground level as he took two steps backward. He gave it the once over and then proclaimed. "Best I've ever gotten." I certainly couldn't dispute that. I hadn't seen them all, but it was difficult to believe anything could be as bad as the four previous trees I'd seen. I picked up the front end of the tree and Will the rear as we started back through the red mud and snow up the hill to the car.

The first time I really ever met Will was four years before when he was putting up his tree. I was ten then, and the car had let me out in front of the ball park. As I walked across the parking lot to the stadium, I had seen this tree setting up on top of the grandstand roof. Even for a ten-year-old I could tell it didn't look so good, and beneath it blowing in the wind was an old piece of canvas with "Merry Xmas" written on it in faded red and green paint.

Oh, sure, I'd seen Will maybe at a couple of family reunions when I was younger, but family reunions were something my mother made me go to, and I sure didn't want to meet all those people. I'd go back and play with Cousin Billy's war toys or something so I didn't have to be with the adults. And then when they told me I was going to live with my Uncle Will for a couple of months I didn't know what to think. You see, I really hated baseball then, and all I knew was that this uncle worked for a baseball team. But I'd lived with so many relatives in the past couple of years, I figured another one wouldn't matter.

And here I was this little runny nosed ten-year-old walking across a field to a baseball park, not really knowing what to think other than what an awful looking Christmas tree that was on the roof, when this voice calls down from the roof. "Hurry, Hurry. The tree's slipping... on the roof, hurry up!" and I looked up and there was this man trying to tie the tree to something. I recognized him as my Uncle Will, and I ran in the stadium and up to the roof just in time to grab one end of the tree to keep it from slipping down to the ground.

I got to thinking about that as Will and I tied the tree on the roof. The snow hadn't stopped and now was coming down much harder and sticking to the roads. We tied the tree to the chicken-wire screen that stood about four foot high on the back of the grandstand roof. It was placed there to keep foul balls from rolling off the roof into the hands of boys waiting outside, but I think Will saw its chief function being to hold up the tree. The "Merry Xmas" sign had been thrown away last year when a high wind had ripped the "Merry" from "Xmas" and Will decided it would be impossible to patch. I was getting pretty cold, but Will was singing the "Twelve Days of Christmas," only he didn't know past the first five, and it was getting sort of repetitious.

We had put the lights on, and the tree was steady, and Will had gone to the press box to flick on the lights when he called me. The roof covered most of the grandstand and the press box was on the top front of the roof, but Will was just standing to one side of it looking down at the field. "Geez," I thought. "Here's Will so eager to see his tree with lights, and now he's stopped to stare at his ball park." I was getting pretty wet, but I shivered up to where he was standing and looked down on the field. I guess the snow had been coming down for three hours, and Will was going on about it being the most beautiful sight he'd ever seen.

I stood with him for a few minutes, and I did have to admit it was a big improvement for the stadium. The left field bleachers were normally dirty concrete, stained brown by years of shoes, tobacco juice, and spilled Coca-cola. Now, they were a pure white, and it looked as if a solid white cushion covered the entire section, instead of the splintery rotten boards I knew to be under the snow. And the field did look as good as it could, for yesterday it had been only ruts and dead grass, and now it was solid white and perfectly even except for the little hump of the mound. It was difficult to believe the old park could be transformed into something really beautiful.

19

The only trouble was that I was still cold and wet, and we hadn't plugged the lights in for the tree. I left Will on the roof and went into the press box and turned the switch. Only a couple of bulbs were out on the lights and I changed them, and then I went back and got Will. I dragged him out into the parking lot, and I guess Will had been right. Maybe this was the best tree ever, which wasn't saying much, but the falling snow and the colored lights made it actually look Christmassy, and I really wasn't that mad that it was snowing.

I was originally supposed to stay with Will only a couple of months until my Aunt Bertha could move into a new house and have enough room for me, but the two months were now in the fourth year. At first they'd figured it wouldn't be good for me to stay too long with Will, him being a bachelor and keeping all those weird hours running a ball club. But it had worked out OK, and Aunt Bertha really didn't mind. She said it might be good for me to spend a summer working in the ball park, and I'd ended up never leaving.

Staying with Will was different than it had been staying with other relatives. It was more like living with Will than staying. When I left home and started moving around to different relatives, it was always as if they were doing a big favor for you. I could never get over the feeling I was a guest with everyone being just too concerned with me. I was seven or eight then, and sometimes I'd cry. It was no big deal, but they'd be all worried and come quietly in and wonder if they could do anything. Well, they could have just left me alone, because I'd get over it and all, but then I'd get to feeling guilty if I cried. Oh, not that they weren't nice. I just never felt at home with anyone until I moved in with Will.

My father left us when I was five, and for a while my mother worked to get enough money to support us. But it was hard to find any sort of decent job, and finally she had to sell the house and move in with my grandmother. The house wasn't that big for a seven-year-old and my grandmother wasn't well enough to have a kid around, and so the rest of the family said they'd take care of me. I think they were happy not to have to take care of my grandmother.

I'm not sure how Will viewed my living with him, but that was why I liked it so much. When I came to stay with him, it was as if I'd always lived there, and he didn't change anything for me. He let me hang around the ball park, and I even did some of his work for him. Will had gone to college for a couple of years and studied English, but he wasn't that good with math. I'd always been good with figures, and one day that first year Will was trying to figure up his receipts for the previous year. He was having trouble, and I ended up doing them for him. After that I did most of his figuring and tickets out at the ball park.

Two or three times a year I'd go down to the eastern part of the state and visit my mother. It was always good to see her. But I guess I considered my home was here with Will. I think my mother really liked that I ended up with Will. He was the youngest in the family, there were seven kids, and my mother always seemed closest to him. Whenever he came east with me, Will would always kid around with her, and she liked it and had more life when he was around. Some of my other aunts and uncles didn't think that much of Will, saying he'd never grown up. But I think they might have been jealous, for they were always so serious which was why it was difficult living with them. Occasionally, one of my aunts would write Will and ask if I could come and spend a month or so with them, but I think most of them were glad it worked out so well for Will and me. I know there were getting to be some arguments over who I was going to stay with next, and let me tell you, some of my cousins made me sick.

"Tom, you know, this house is missing something. We probably should have gotten a tree for it."

Now here I was trying to listen to Ray Reeve and Bill Currie broadcast the game, and Carolina was really having trouble with West Virginia, and he starts in on a Christmas tree for the house.

21

"Will, we won't even be here Christmas. And we've never had one before."

"I know. But we'll be here part of Christmas Day. Sure would look good to get one."

I'd have to do some quick talking to get him out of having a tree for the house. I could just imagine what sort of tree he'd pick out. The place would probably look like a forest. "Will, they'll have a tree down east. And we don't have any decorations. And besides, it's too late now."

"Maybe, you're right, but I sure would like something."

I knew what the problem was. The snow had changed to rain in the afternoon, and most of it was melting. With no chance for a white Christmas, I guess Will had started thinking about putting a tree in the house to give it a Christmas feel. "Will, we've really got our own tree down at the ball park. Why don't we drive down there now and see how the lights look at night."

"Good idea."

And so we drove through the slush about a mile to the ball park. Besides, Carolina was about to lose, and I didn't want to hear that. We parked the car a good distance from the park and sat on the fender and stared at our Christmas tree on the roof. I guess people driving by must have thought it funny to see these two people sitting on their car, looking at a Christmas tree on the top of a ball park roof in rain with slushy snow at their shoes. But it was so pretty and peaceful, it seemed hard to think that things could ever be any different. And yet, even then, there was something behind the outfield fence that was to change everything, and it would be the last time Will and I ever sat and looked at the Christmas tree on the roof.

2

The drive has taken you into the city, and you make more than one wrong turn. It is different, but still there are some of the same streets, and you gradually make your way to what was the center of the city. But the downtown is no longer the center, and it is now only a collection of empty buildings, seedy clothing stores, and a few last hangers-on. There is much to look at, but somehow your mind keeps wandering back to that final year. There is something that you can't put your finger on, and it bothers you. Is that why you have never made a trip back? Is that what is telling you to turn around and continue your journey? What is wrong? It is the fence that started it. Somehow the fence at the park is involved, and the day it fell down is when everything started falling apart.

"TOM, don't spatter that paint. If we get any on the floor, we'll have to start scraping."

You know, sometimes Will could really gripe me. I mean, did he think I wanted to spatter paint on the floor? Heck, I wanted to scrape that floor less than he did. In fact, I didn't even want to be painting, and if anybody ought to be worried about spattering, it was Will. I'd seen him kick a bucket of paint over, something I'd never done. We shouldn't have been painting at all. It wasn't our job, or really Will's, but once he got something in his mind, he was going to do it. We'd painted the two previous years, but why did he have to pick a time when I had only two days left on my Christmas vacation? When I asked him about it, he said the day was perfect for painting, clear and sunny, which meant the walls of the stadium wouldn't sweat and the paint would stick. The day was also perfect for going to the playground and shooting my new basketball. Monty had called up, wanting to shoot, but no, I had to paint.

Christmas had turned out better than I'd expected. Sometimes it can really be a let down, particularly in our family where everybody goes down to my grandmother's for a few hours on Christmas Day. You end up seeing people you don't want to see, and some of the relatives give crummy presents. Then you have to write a thank you letter when you'd just as soon not have been given the socks anyway because they're so awful.

I'd been trying to sleep late on Christmas morning, but Will woke me up for the long drive down to the eastern part of the state. At breakfast he brought in my presents and sure enough there was a basketball. There wasn't much doubt it was a basketball, even though Will had tried to wrap it. Most of the time

Will wasn't much good at anything with his hands, and his trying to wrap that round basketball must have been a sight. There was more Scotch tape on the tissue paper than paper itself. He'd also gotten me a couple of shirts from Roth's, button-down collars, that really did look good even if he did buy them at a discount. Finally, there was a belt and a couple of books (paperback westerns that I was reading all the time).

I felt a little bad because all I had for Will was a wallet. But he seemed pleased and made a big to-do right at the breakfast table of transferring his cards and money from the old wallet (which was falling apart and looking like it had a bad case of the mange). After that I didn't feel that bad, mainly because Will looked so stupid transferring all that stuff at breakfast.

It took us about two and a half hours to make the drive east, which was about average. The snow had melted the previous day and there wasn't even a hint of a white Christmas. The drive might have been prettier if the snow had stayed, for about all you had to look at in that part of the state were scrub pines and run-down farms.

My mother greeted us at the door of my grandmother's, and I was really glad to see her. She looked older or maybe just tired, but she hugged and kissed me, and we sat down and talked for maybe an hour (it was always easy to talk to my mother). Then most of the other relatives started arriving, and I had to say hello to them. But they weren't as bad as I remembered. My grandmother was having one of her good days, so it turned out all right. Most of the relatives who lived nearby brought food, and my mother had baked a turkey, and although Cousin Billy got sick and had to throw up (he made it to the bathroom), I thought it was all good and sure much better than Will's cooking. We didn't stay too long after the meal because of the drive back, although I don't remember much of the drive because I was sleeping most of the way.

"Will, how much longer you think this will take?"

"Can't really say. We may want to start on that other bathroom with the weather being so good."

I knew he was going to say that. It looked like I was never going to be able to use that basketball. I just couldn't understand Will's way of thinking. I mean, who cared what the bathrooms looked like at a ball park? You knew automatically that they would be grungy. Ball park bathrooms are supposed to be bad. But not Will's. Each year he'd go through the same routine of painting them, and he wasn't even getting paid for it, and it sure wasn't his job. I don't even think the fans cared that much, because at the end of the season they'd look bad again and people would have written on the walls and all that stuff. And the girls' bathroom, you just wouldn't believe. Will went to extra trouble in there, and he even put up some awful looking curtains to try to make the place look decent, but it didn't matter. I'd tell the guys at school some of the stuff they'd write on the walls, and I know most of them thought I was lying. But it was true. Not that I go around sneaking and looking in the girls' bathroom, but with painting it and during the season emptying the trash, I just knew. Once I suggested to Will that we just forget about painting it and they'd run out of space to write. But he wouldn't hear of it.

"Tom, painting the bathrooms is almost like the start of spring. Before you know it, the days will start getting warm, the grass will start getting green, and the umpire will yell, 'Play ball!' "

Now, can you get over a grown man talking like that? It must have been the fumes from the paint or something. But I guess it figured. Will was the general manager of the Centerville Owls of the Carolina League, and he took it as his full-time job to promote baseball and to do anything he could for the Owls. The only problem was that he wasn't paid full time. And that's one of the reasons this painting made me mad. His salary from the big league club didn't start until the middle of January, and here he was, wasting my day and his, painting.

Probably this will take some explaining because I guess everybody's not as up on the Centerville Owls as I was, but I'll try to make it simple. The Centerville Owls were a minor league baseball team in the Class B Carolina League and were owned by a major league team. The reason the big league club owned the Owls was that they hoped some of the players would get good enough so they could play in the major leagues. Only most of our players weren't even good enough to play for the Owls. Will's job was to run all aspects of the Owls except for the team on the field. That was the field manager's job. Will sent out contracts to players in January, sold advertising for the fence signs and scorebook, sold season tickets, spoke to civic clubs, hired ushers and ticket salesmen, and just made sure people were coming to see the team play. I think he was pretty good because the Owls usually led the league in attendance although they hadn't won a pennant in a long time, and Will had been there five years. There was a lot more to it, but that's how I'd explain it if some dumb girl in school asked me what Will did. Anyway, he was paid mid-January through September, and we were painting when his salary hadn't started.

From October through Christmas, Will worked down at Roth's Fine Men's Clothiers, and that's how I got those shirts for Christmas. Even at the clothing store, you'd have thought Will was still working for the baseball team, because all he did was talk about the Owls. And during those months off, he'd come out to the ball park three or four days a week and pick up the mail and make a few phone calls and try to renew the fence signs on the outfield wall. He never told me what the big league club paid him, but I'm sure it wasn't what he was worth.

"Tom, I think we've about got it in here. Fine looking rest room, fine looking. Now, let's give the other a start."

"What about the colored rest rooms?"

"I think we can wait until next weekend on those, unless you want to start on those later today."

"Come off it, Will. I don't even want to get started on the men's room. I'm going to have the only basketball in the history of captivity that's never been dribbled."

"I see where your boys finally lost one. No championship this year."

Carolina had lost a game, and Will was rubbing it in every chance. I wasn't taking it so good, either. "Just you wait. Come March, they'll be national champs again."

28

We started dragging the drop cloths into the men's room and setting things up as Will kept talking about Carolina losing a basketball game. I tried to change the subject. "Will, why doesn't the city do this painting? It's their ball park."

"Tom, I wish I knew the answer. They just don't do much of anything to help out here."

The Centerville Owls leased Centerville Stadium from the city for a nominal fee each year. The park had been built in the twenties when baseball was booming in the south, but thirty years later it was pretty run down, and the city didn't really seem to care about it anymore. I couldn't understand it. I read in the papers where the city was having a bond issue to build a coliseum like Charlotte, but they never spent any money on the ball park.

Centerville was the fifth largest city in the state, behind Charlotte, Greensboro, Winston-Salem, and Raleigh, and the people were hoping in the next census the town might reach a hundred thousand in population. The town wasn't that much different from any of the other cities in that part of the state, being built up around textile mills. Textiles were still the largest industry, although lately furniture and tobacco had moved into the area. The city was located on the main line of the Southern Railway. Sometimes when I didn't have much to do, I'd go down to the tracks with my best friends, Monty Oxendine and Donald Perkins, and put pennies on the tracks to watch the trains flatten the coins. I heard it was a federal offense to do that, but we went ahead and did it anyway.

As might be expected, Centerville was located in the center of the state. It was not dead center, but center enough to be called Centerville since I guess they'd never had a famous enough citizen to name it after. There were three movie theaters downtown (in the colored section of town there were two theaters, but we couldn't go there), a movie theater in the mill village, two drive-ins, and one bowling alley. I heard where up north they had bowling alleys with machines that put down the pins automatically, but not at the Dixie Bowling Emporium. We'd roll on Saturday morning when they had the youth league, and colored men would put up the pins for us. Monty and Donald and I rolled duck pins (nobody rolled anything else—the big balls were for twerps), and when Donald was having a bad day, he'd forget about trying to knock down pins. Instead, he'd see if he could throw a ball hard enough to make the pin jump up and hit a pin boy. I never saw him do it, but that didn't keep Donald from trying.

About the only thing the City of Centerville did for the stadium was to supply a groundskeeper. His real name was something like Harrison Jamieson Wilson, but I had never heard him called that. "Piedmont" was what everybody called him. He had started out at the ball park when it had first been built, and he'd never left. The Owls were in the Piedmont League then, and I guess that's where he got his name. You'd have thought it was still 1925 the way he fixed the field. He was so slow sometimes you wanted to scream, but each year he was back. It didn't bother Will a bit that the games sometimes would be five minutes late starting because Piedmont was still out dragging the infield.

Most of the time Piedmont was all right, but there were other times too. Not that Piedmont and I weren't friends. I helped him sometimes on the field, but he had this problem. He'd sort of sidle up to me and say, "You know, Tom, a man gets mighty thirsty," and I'd know he was drunk and want me to go to the concession stand and bring him a beer. Here it was illegal for me to get beer, but if I let Piedmont go up to the stand, somebody might see that he was drunk. Then they'd have to complain to the city or Will, and Piedmont might get fired. So I'd go up to the concession stand and tell Stewart, the concession manager, that the team needed a few beers for the clubhouse. Stewart knew what I was getting them for, but he'd go ahead and let me have them. I'd take them down to Piedmont so he could get a little more drunk during the game. It was all right to get drunk during a game, I guess, for there wasn't any work for Piedmont to do. Once we had a rainout when Piedmont was drunk, and he had to go cover the pitcher's mound with the tarp. It didn't get done so good.

I used to ask Will why he kept Piedmont. He didn't pay Piedmont, the city did, but I'm sure if Will had gone to the city he'd have been able to get them to change groundskeepers. But Will said he wasn't sure the city would change Piedmont. He said they probably couldn't get anybody to work as cheap. And he said that Piedmont knew more about that field than anybody alive. The players never complained about the playing surface. And then Will would get in one of his moods like he was giving a speech to the Jaycees or Rotary Club, and he'd say, "Tom, how can you replace Piedmont? Why he's as much a part of this stadium as the brick walls, the seats, and the dugouts. You'd be doing away with the very soul of this park if you let Piedmont go." By this stage I was always sorry I'd asked the question, what with Will feeling that part of his job as the Centerville G.M. was to keep Piedmont around.

It was funny how Will became general manager of a minor league baseball team. Most of the other general managers in the league were old guys who used to be players. They all smoked big cigars and sat around grumbling how things weren't as good now as they were in the old days. Will had never played baseball, and if the truth were known, he wasn't much of an athlete. When I first moved in with him, he'd sometimes play catch with me, and you could just tell by the way he threw and caught that he hadn't played much.

When Will dropped out of college, he got a job with an insurance company, and this company sent him to Centerville. It turned out that Will was just a whiz selling insurance, or at least that's what I hear because he never talked much about it. They thought he was really going places. But when the Korean War broke out, Will volunteered and was sent as a medic to Korea. I've heard it from a couple of people who say when Will came back he just wasn't the same. Not that he was really different, but when he went back with his old insurance company, he just didn't sell like he had before.

31

About the same time, the Centerville Owls were really in trouble. It was 1952 and baseball teams were folding all over the country with people staying home and watching "I Love Lucy" and Milton Berle rather than going out to the parks. The owner of the Owls decided he'd had enough, and he moved the club to High Point-Thomasville (the Hi-Toms). This shook up a lot of people in Centerville, for the Owls had been in town for almost fifty years, even during World War II when most teams disbanded. Some of the local citizens formed a committee to keep baseball in town, and Will was put in charge. He had always gone to the games before he went in the service, and even at the last of '52 when he was being discharged, he was at all the games. Well, Will went out and took pledges for tickets and advertising, and he went to a major league club that was looking for a place to put a Class B club. He showed them all the money that had been pledged for a club in Centerville, and they decided to place their club in the town. In fact, they were so impressed with what Will had done, they asked him if he would like to be the business manager. With the insurance going slowly and everything, there was no way he could refuse. After that he never thought of doing anything else.

I asked Will sometimes why he didn't work somewhere where he could make more money, and he'd always say, "Tom, there are some things money can't buy, and money can't buy a warm Carolina summer night with a ball game, a box of popcorn, and green grass on a field." Will had this thing about green grass, even though ours usually turned brown in August.

We were halfway through the men's room when Will spoke up. "Tom, this is going mighty slow. I think maybe we'll stop, and it'll give you time to get to the playground and shoot a little basketball." That sounded like a fine idea, and I indicated as much to Will. He continued talking. "You know, Maggie and I are going to see 'Around the World in Eighty Days' tonight. How'd you like to come along with us?" Normally, I tried to stay away from Will and his lady friends. Who wants some fourteen-year-old tagging along when you're out on a date? I wasn't that dumb. But I wanted to see the movie, and besides, Maggie was OK. I told Will I'd be happy to go along with them.

We were closing up the paint cans and putting the brushes in turpentine and doing all that messy stuff that makes painting work when we heard Piedmont shuffling along the passageway. There was no mistaking Piedmont's walk except this time it seemed much faster. He came into the men's room.

"You better come quick, Mr. Will. It's the big, funny one. He hurt."

"How bad?" Will had put his paint brush down and was already heading out of the men's room.

"He's bleeding. Don' know how bad."

Will looked back at me. "Tom, go get my kit. We'll be on the field."

I didn't want to miss anything. I rushed to the office and in Will's desk drawer pulled out a small first aid kit. Will and Piedmont were halfway across the outfield when I reached the field, and I was running as fast as I could to catch up with them. A huge section of the outfield fence had been pulled down, and I could hear somebody moaning. I knew it was Millard.

I caught up with Will and Piedmont just as they went through the new hole in the outfield fence, and both of them started lifting a huge piece of fence off the man lying in the weeds that were growing behind the fence. When the boards were off, Will took the bag from me and went to the man who was still moaning. It was hard to tell how badly he was hurt, but Will leaned over him and started looking at a cut which had blood all around it.

The thing about Will was he usually looked like he couldn't do anything. He'd fumble around, and you'd have thought he had five thumbs. Except I'd seen him when he needed to do something in a hurry, and it was crucial. You'd have sworn it was a different person. It was the same way this time. Will was over Millard calming him down as he looked at him. You'd have thought Will knew what he was doing, which I suppose he did, what with him being a medic in Korea and all. He was talking quietly to the big man as he worked on him, and pretty soon there wasn't any bleeding and Millard stopped moaning. Things seemed in good shape when Will turned to me.

"Tom, how about going to the office and calling the councilman." Again, I started the long run across the outfield.

I suppose I should explain Millard, although I kind of wish I didn't know him. The trouble was he came around the ball park all the time, and there wasn't much I could do about it. You see, Millard was a little crazy. Will told me to say retarded, but that's close to crazy. He couldn't talk good at all, and sometimes you could understand him but most times you couldn't. And he walked funny and looked funny. Personally, I'd rather have not had anything to do with him. I guess he was harmless, and I never heard of him hurting anybody, except you could get him really mad if you called him "Dumbo." I'd never called him that, but I'd seen some boys from over in the mill village call him that once at the park, and Will had to come out and lead Millard into the office.

He was Councilman Waller's son, and Councilman Waller was the chief baseball backer in town. The councilman was also a druggist, and he had a drug store that had the best cherry-Pepsi's in Centerville. I suppose the councilman didn't feel good about having a son who was retarded, but he treated him just like he was normal, or as normal as you can treat somebody who's like Millard. Each year Millard was the bat boy for the Owls, and it always looked odd to me. I haven't mentioned it, but Millard must have been twenty-five or thirty and was really big.

I used to think the reason that Will let Millard hang around the park might be because he was the councilman's son. But I don't think so anymore. Will's kind of soft on certain things, and I imagine he'd have let Millard hang around the park no matter whose son he was.

When I got back to the office I gave a call down to the drug store, and the councilman was in. He said he'd be right out. I hung around the office, and it took maybe five minutes for Mr.

34

Waller to show up. He was concerned and everything, but I told him Will had things fixed up, and as near as I could tell Millard was OK. That seemed to make him feel better, and as we walked across the outfield, he put his arm around my shoulders and called me "son" and thanked me for taking so much time with Millard. To be honest, I tried to take as little time as possible with Millard, but I thanked him anyway. He was the sort of person who always put his arm around your shoulders and called you "son."

We walked through the section of the fence that had just been torn down, and I could see that Millard was on his feet and doing just fine. The councilman put his arm around his son's shoulders and scolded him quietly. "Now, Millard, you know you shouldn't be fooling around and leaving your mother at home worried over where you've gone."

He turned to Will. "How is he, Will?"

"He was more scared than anything. There's a cut on his scalp and a bruise on his forehead, but nothing serious as far as I can tell. Probably be a good idea to take him by the hospital for a tetanus shot and a little more checking."

"How'd it happen?"

"I'm not really sure. The fence isn't that old that it would fall down just like that. But it seems like Millard was climbing around it when it fell."

Millard was making some sounds and pointing to the area of the fence, and I could see that Piedmont was going over to check it out. Will yelled over to Piedmont to watch out and not let any more fence fall, but the groundskeeper was lifting up one of the large sheet metal sections that had fallen. I'm not sure what Piedmont hoped to accomplish by lifting it, but when he had raised it halfway, he looked underneath and gave a low moan. He looked over to the group around Millard.

"Mr. Will, you better come look."

Will left Millard, and together he and Piedmont lifted up the big section of metal and threw it to one side. From where I was standing, it looked as if one of the support posts holding the

35

fencing had completely been pulled up from the ground. There was a good deal of loose earth and debris nearby. We'd had a good amount of rain that winter, which may have accounted for the dirt being so loose, but in the loose earth, something was sticking out. Piedmont and Will were staring at the object.

Normally, I guess you could say I've got pretty good curiosity and I'm into about everything at the ball park, but I knew something wasn't right the way Will and Piedmont were looking. For some reason, I started shaking. Will looked over my way and called out.

"Tom, how about going back to the office and giving the police a call to come on out here."

I should have asked why, but I wasn't sure I wanted to know. Will looked over to the councilman as I started to leave. "Mr. Waller, I guess maybe we should keep Millard here for a little bit until the police come. There're going to be some questions. You see, there's a body under this fence."

I ran as quick as I could to the phone.

3

The body. You wonder at how you had forgotten it over the years. It must have been the familiar sights as you came in that triggered the memory. It was so important in your life that year, and yet now it is only a dim recollection. You continue driving through the city, remembering a few landmarks but more amazed at the changes. There is a realization that this isn't the same town you left, that they have only taken the name of a place that was important at one time. But there are certain things that bring back a poignancy that is hard to explain. Maybe you will spend a little more time than you had planned. It might be good to try to find out what really happened that year. And the body, the dead man? Did they ever find out who did it?

"HEY, Tom, they find out about the body yet?"
"Naw. Police said it'd been buried at least six months. No identification or anything. They had to send it to Raleigh for tests."

"When they supposed to find out?"

"Don't know if they ever will."

"Who do you think it was? Some gangster or something?"

I didn't answer and instead poked at the fire. The thing about Donald was that he could drive a subject into the ground. Ever since they found the body, that was all he could talk about. I poked the fire again, and a blaze sprung up as I got closer to warm my hands. It was really cold that day, and that's why we didn't go to shoot my basketball. I was with my two friends, Monty Oxendine and Donald Perkins. We're all in the same class at school and, during the season, we all work at the ball park. I'm in charge of tickets for Will plus I work in the club house shining players' shoes, Donald sells cokes in the stands, and Monty is the scoreboard boy. The scoreboard boy sits on top of the scoreboard and drops numbers into the inning slot whenever anybody scores a run. He's also in charge of the owl.

I probably should explain the owl, because that's the reason we went over to the park that day and were behind the fence building a fire. It's really sort of dumb, the owl, but it was another of Will's ideas and Monty was in charge of it. When Will saved the Centerville ball club in '52, he thought the park needed something to liven it up, and he came up with the idea for this giant metal owl to be the team mascot. I don't know who built it for him, but it's attached to the back of the fence right next to the scoreboard. The metal owl has hinges on its feet and it hangs upside down behind the fence with a long rope stretching to a pulley on the scoreboard. Whenever any Owl hits a home run or does something good, the scoreboard operator has to jump off the scoreboard, pulling on the rope, and this giant eight-foot-owl comes standing up on top of the fence. I mean, it's really goofy, but the fans like it.

That's Monty's job, to pull the owl up, and he likes that stupid metal bird almost as much as Will does. That's why we went behind the fence that day. Monty had this idea that he wanted to install lights in the owl's eyes so they could light up when he pulled up the bird. When Monty first thought up the idea, I didn't like it at all, but Will went right along with it, and Monty wanted to get started so it would be ready for the season.

The three of us had ridden our bikes over to Centerville Stadium after school so Monty could begin making plans for the owl's eyes. There wasn't much for Donald and me to do so we were generally goofing around. The fence had still not been repaired, and Donald and I collected some of the old wood supports from the fence and put them in a pile and started a fire to keep warm. Of course, Will wasn't around the ball park that afternoon, because I don't really think he would have approved of us starting a fire.

I was sitting near the fire while Monty was over at the owl trying to figure out how to wire the eyes as Donald poked around the area where the body had been found. I sure couldn't understand Donald. I still got shaky when I thought of a body being there, but Donald was kicking the dirt and seeing if he could find anything. The police had been all over the area, so there wasn't much of anything that Donald could find. In fact, the police had found what they thought was the murder weapon, an old piece of iron pipe, but that didn't keep Donald from looking all over.

Well, with Donald talking about the body, and me not wanting to hear it, I brought up the Lumbees and the Klan, mainly just to change the subject. It had been all over the newspapers that weekend, but neither Monty nor Donald had read much about it. I figured since Monty was one-half Lumbee he should know, and Donald always seemed to get a kick out of the Klan and the white sheets they wore. I wasn't that much of an expert, but Will and I had gone through a pretty good discussion Sunday morning as I was reading the paper.

"Hey, Will, did you read what the Indians did in Maxton?"
"No, what?"
"The Klan was holding a rally, and some Indians came and shot things up and drove the Klan away."
"Anybody hurt?"
"Nah. The Klan was protesting some Indians moving next to a couple of white families, and they burned crosses in the Indian front yards a few days before the rally. Made the Indians really mad."
"The Indians must have been the Lumbees."
"Yeah, how'd you know?"
"They live down in Robeson County. About the only group of Indians who'd do something like that."

I kept reading, but there wasn't much more except to describe the incident and how the Klan ran. So we started talking about the Lumbees. Will sometimes surprised me. Sometimes you'd think he didn't know much more than his baseball team and didn't care about what else was going on in the world. But I guess he did, for he sure knew a little about the Lumbees.

It seemed as if the Lumbees weren't like any other tribe in the nation and didn't live on a reservation or anything. I'd been to the mountains once where the Cherokees lived, and most of them lived on a reservation and sold blankets and trinkets to the tourists. But the Lumbees just lived in the southeastern part of the state and worked and farmed like anybody else. Some of the elected officials like sheriffs and mayors were Indian, and you couldn't much tell them from anybody else.

Nobody really knew where the tribe had originated, but some legends, according to Will, had them being descendants of the "Lost Colony." That was the first English colony in the New World, founded in the sixteenth century on the outer banks of North Carolina. The colony disappeared without a trace, but over a hundred years later when white settlers started going into the interior of North Carolina, they found a tribe of Indians living in what was going to be Robeson County. These Indians were different, for they farmed like white men, and some of them had blue eyes and English names, and they lived in log cabins which no Indians lived in anywhere.

The newspaper said that the county had 40,000 whites, 30,000 Indians, and 25,000 Negro population. According to Will the Indians and whites had been living together and marrying each other since the Civil War, but they had a three-way segregation system in the schools with separate facilities for Indians, whites, and colored.

"How come they don't have the Lumbees going to school with the whites?" With Monty being part Lumbee, I still went to school with him.

"Don't really know. Some people just like to pass laws."

"You think they'll ever try to integrate the ball park?" Of course, Centerville Stadium had separate seating for colored people with colored rest rooms, water fountains, and all that.

"I doubt it. It's been segregated so long I don't think anybody would go to the trouble to try to change it."

We talked a little longer about it as I ate my eggs. It was sort of interesting to think about. The past fall all the newspapers had written on the integration of Central High School in Little Rock, Arkansas. But there sure wasn't much integration in North Carolina. In a way the ball park was integrated. The wives of the colored ball players sat with the white wives in the box seat section, and Mr. Johnson, who was colored and our ticket taker, would always go up in the main grandstand after he'd finished working and sit with his railroad friends. He'd retired from the Southern about five years before, and he sat with the white railroad retirees.

About the only way integration had touched Centerville was with the buses. Just last year all the public buses had taken down the signs that said, "Colored sit from the rear. White sit from the front." Personally, I was glad they'd done away with the laws on the buses although it was a little late for me. When I first moved to Centerville I had never ridden on a bus, and I went to the elementary school every morning on the big Duke Power Company buses. Like a dumb ten-year-old, the one thing I really wanted to do was sit on that big wide seat in the back. The motor was right under the seat, and someone had told me it got all hot and you could feel the engine vibrate. But the sign on the bus said I had to sit from the front. I never got to sit on that big wide seat. Of course, now that I was fourteen I didn't ride buses anymore, and in a couple of years I'd be old enough to drive a car anyway.

We were still sitting behind the fence, and as Monty kept working on his owl, Donald started talking about the Lumbees, the Ku Klux Klan, and the "niggers." I got to thinking about the word "nigger." Will didn't like me to use it, and the truth was I didn't say it very well. In a way, it was like cussing. You could always tell the guys who'd cussed before and those who hadn't. It just didn't sound quite right when somebody cussed and they didn't know how. About the only word I could use and feel comfortable with was "damn," and I always wondered how you could use those other words enough times to sound like you always said them. Donald had a friend named Gerald who had quit high school at seventeen and joined the Navy. One day when we were fooling around Gerald showed up. We just couldn't believe some of the words he was using. I had never even heard some of the words before, but there was no doubting they were cuss words. We were really impressed. The most important thing was that he sounded like he had been using them all his life. Donald ran around with Gerald all that week when he was home on leave, and the next week he tried some of the words out on me. They just never did sound right when Donald used them.

It really was turning into a good afternoon. The fire was warm, Donald was running his mouth, and Monty was all excited about his owl. He even came up with an idea that sounded good to me. As he was measuring for the eyes, he began talking about getting an old auto horn for the owl's voice that would go "aaaaaoooooooogggggaaahhhh." I had to admit it might add something. We all three were standing around the fire talking about what a voice for the owl might do when we heard someone yelling from the grandstand.

I looked up and saw a colored woman with a broom, waving the handle at us. We could barely make out the voice, but there wasn't much doubt what she was saying. The three of us quickly started to kick the fire out. Donald was muttering "Damn Elmira," but he was kicking the fire harder than anybody. We started in toward the grandstand once the fire was out, and as we reached the infield, the colored woman's voice became distinct.

"You boys. What you think you doin' out there, burnin' up city property? Tom, what yo' uncle gonna say when he hears you out startin' fires while he's away? You boys got no sense?" She went on like that the whole time we walked to the grandstand, and none of the three of us was saying anything. Not that she was giving us much of a chance to get a word in anyway. You'd have thought Miss Elmira owned the ball park the way she was going on. Both Donald and Monty pretended they were late and had to leave, and they rushed off on their bikes while I had to stay as Miss Elmira kept on talking.

It was always hard for me to figure out how Elmira could boss everybody around. I could have asked Will except she bossed him around, and he was the general manager. As near as I could figure out, Miss Elmira's official job was to be the maid. Well, that's what other people called colored women who cleaned up and did the bathrooms and all that stuff. But I sure never thought of her as a maid. Most people probably thought she was in charge of the ball park the way she acted.

Will's thing about ball park bathrooms was the reason Miss Elmira was working at the stadium in the first place. For those who don't know, ball park bathrooms are the worst things ever created when it comes to cleaning. I know from experience, because the first year I came to live with Will he had me clean them sometimes. I'd pick up the paper and pour a little disinfect-

44

ant in the commodes, and that was my idea of cleaning them. It was really Piedmont's job to clean them, but if you can believe it, he was worse than I was. By June of that first year in Centerville, the bathrooms were smelling pretty rank. Don't get me wrong. I'd been around to some of the other parks in the league, and their rest rooms were worse than ours ever were that first year. But ours certainly would have been in the second division of league toilets. Fans started complaining, and by mid-season Will was talking about hiring somebody special just to clean the rest rooms. I said I thought it was a good idea, because it would mean I didn't have to do it anymore.

One day out of the blue, Will received this telephone call from some colored woman asking if he needed anybody to clean up the rest rooms or do any other work. Will is sort of superstitious. If the team's on a winning streak he'll keep wearing the same shirt, and he'll do all those other stupid things people do when they think their luck is running good. Now, Will took this phone call as a sign, and although he usually had people come in for an interview before hiring them, he hired the telephone caller on the spot.

It turned out to be Miss Elmira, and she started working that afternoon. She was about five feet tall and nearly as wide, and when she saw the bathrooms, she started telling Will they were disgraceful. She found out we didn't have any Ajax and our mops were falling apart, and right on the first day she'd been hired she started bossing Will, telling him to go out and buy all that stuff. Will was just chuckling, saying, "Tom, boy, we've got ourselves a good one," and sure enough, he went right out and bought all that stuff the next day.

OK, so the bathrooms were clean, but now there was another problem. I was afraid to use them. It was in July, and I was down the right field bleacher side, chasing foul balls from batting practice, when I heard this awful commotion coming from the colored men's room. I could hear Miss Elmira screaming, and as I looked over in that direction, I saw three colored kids come running out, scared to death, with Miss Elmira in hot pursuit, trying to hit them with her broom. It wasn't much of a race, Miss

45

Elmira didn't have much staying power, but I wandered over and asked her what had happened.

"Them boys was messin' up my bathrooms 'fo' the game start. I'm gonna see Mr. Will and get locks for them doors." Sure enough, she marched right down to the office and demanded that Will put locks and hasps on the rest room doors so no one could use them before the game started. Now this seemed kind of stupid to me. I was taught that if you've got to go, you've got to go. Whether a baseball game was going on didn't have much to do with it. So I couldn't believe it the next day when I saw Will drilling away on the bathroom doors.

"Will," I asked. "Whatcha doin'?" I knew, but I wanted to make sure.

"Tom, I've got to get these locks on the doors for Elmira."

"But what if somebody has to use the john before the game starts?"

"No problem, Tom. We'll open them an hour before game time, and we'll have the key in the office if someone needs to use them before then. All they'll have to do is come by the office."

It sounded good, but it didn't work that way. Many's the time I was about to bust but didn't go for fear of messing up Elmira's bathrooms. And I know for a fact that Will himself was afraid to use the key, for I'd see him fidgeting around, and as soon as the front gates were opened an hour before game time, he'd rush to the bathroom to use it himself.

Elmira had wound down about our starting the fire behind the fence, and we were both sitting in the office as she waited for Will to get back so he could pay her. Finally, her husband drove up and honked the horn, and she decided to leave anyway. I was just as happy because I was sure she would have told Will about the fire and he might have gotten angry. I didn't know where Will was, he was much later than usual, and as Elmira left, she told me to tell Will he could pay her when she stopped by our house on Thursday.

46

When Elmira came to work at the ball park, she didn't stop with cleaning the rest rooms. In a few weeks, she was cleaning the office also, and by the end of the season she was running the concession stand under the colored bleachers. And finally, that fall, she started cleaning our house. Even though I didn't like her being so bossy, her cleaning our house was one of the best things that ever happened to me.

When I first came to live with Will, he wasn't that big on keeping things straight, and I really liked it. Aunt Bertha had been something of a fanatic about things being clean, but Will was pretty casual about it. Occasionally on a Saturday we'd get out the vacuum, but mostly things slid. Toward the end of my first summer in Centerville, some of the relatives came up to visit and see how things were going, and I guess they made some comments about bringing up a boy in conditions like that. Well, Will went and asked Miss Elmira if she could come clean our house, and right then I knew Will wanted me to stay with him permanently. Up until that point, I thought I might be going back to stay with other relatives.

It was 5:30 before Will finally got back to the ball park, and normally I would have ridden my bicycle home to start my homework. But I'd promised Monty I'd ask Will about the horn for his owl, so I had stuck around the office. But I never had the chance that day to ask Will about the owl, for when Will's Studebaker drove up and he came into the office I could tell something was wrong.

"Where you been, Will?"

"Police station, Tom."

"Something the matter?"

"Well, sort of. They found out who the body was."

"They did? Who?"

"Tom, it was your father."

*How much time do you have to chase after a vague memory?
You have important places to go. You turned off the road, it was
just a whim, and now something unpleasant is nagging at your
mind. You might spend a bit longer than you planned, for your
father was murdered, and it would be good to have those doubts
removed. But where can you start? You have forgotten the
names, most of the people from that year. You need something
to jog your memory, and you turn your car toward the old
library. It is not there, they have built a shiny new building, but
finally you reach it. Why is it that you remember so little of what
happened?*

WHEN something good and bad happens, which do you tell first? It's really hard to know. The bad has to do with detectives coming to the school to talk to me. That wasn't really bad in itself, but it was how I got to the principal's office in the first place which was the bad part. And the good wasn't really that great, although I wouldn't have told Will that. In fact, the way he was acting you might have thought it was the greatest thing that ever happened, and for him maybe it was.

Will wasn't home when I got there from school which was good, because I was late getting home which was part of the bad. It was getting close to supper time, and since I knew Will didn't have anything planned, I heated up a can of spaghetti and started eating it as I watched television. I was midway through "Sea Hunt" when Will came in.

"Tom, I think I might be in love."

Now wasn't that something to say! There was only one thing I could do. I turned off the TV and never did find out if the air held out in Lloyd Bridges's tanks. With Will telling me he was in love, it just wouldn't have been right for me to keep watching. I'm not sure what he wanted me to do, but I think he wanted to talk to somebody, and because I was the only person around, I met the qualifications. I went to the refrigerator and came back with a Pepsi as Will paced up and down the living room floor.

"Tom, you know it's hard to believe."

I wasn't sure if I'd be able to take this conversation. Will and girls was a subject I avoided. In the time I'd lived with Will he'd dated several girls, but I wasn't that fond of most of them. Of course, he didn't go after girls the way ball players did, but ball players were different from everybody else in the world. I know when you got older you were supposed to go out with girls and

51

all that, but you wouldn't believe some of the stories the players told in the locker room. At least, I didn't believe all the stories they told. I even knew some of the girls they talked about, and those girls wouldn't do that sort of thing, or I didn't think so.

Will's relations with girls were different. He'd date one a couple of times, but then he'd just seem to lose interest. I know some of the girls still liked him, because they would come to the games like they wanted to see baseball. But they'd get me aside and ask what Will thought of them. I'd just say that Will thought they were real nice. I didn't really know what Will thought of them, because he didn't talk that much about it and never seemed to want to get serious about anybody.

"Tom, the girl is Maggie."

Did he really think I was that dumb? I knew it was something different with her, even before he ever took her out. It was over a year ago, and one night he'd been fidgeting and walking back and forth while I was trying to do some homework in the living room. I knew Will wanted to ask me something, and finally he said could I go down to Hite's and pick up a loaf of bread. Now, we had nearly half a loaf left in the kitchen. I didn't know what it was all about, but I was smart enough to see he didn't want me around. I jumped on my bike and went down to the store that stayed open until 10. When I came back, I could see through a window that Will was on the telephone. I didn't know if he wanted me to go in, but I went in the house anyway. You could tell by the way Will was talking that it was a girl, and I started making noises in the kitchen to make sure he knew I was back. He hurried and hung up and didn't say anything to me, and so I asked him if he'd been talking to a girl. He said maybe.

Now, Will is thirty-one, and you'd think he would be past the stage where he acted like he was seventeen, but the next night you'd have thought it was his first prom. He had a haircut during the day, he shined his shoes which he never does, and he had me check his suit once he dressed to make certain everything looked all right. Right then and there I hoped if I ever started dating girls, I'd never act like that. Was any girl worth it?

52

"Now tell me the truth, Tom. Don't you think Maggie is about the best thing you ever met?"

Well, I did have to admit Maggie was all right. Well, maybe better than all right. She was short and sort of pretty, and she smiled a lot. You couldn't help liking her when she smiled. She'd kid around with me and even tried to hug me once just to embarrass me, which it did. But I really didn't mind the hug that much.

She wasn't like the other girls Will had dated. Will's taste in women ran to ones who wore a lot of makeup and chewed gum. I guess that's why he never got serious. Maggie was different. For one thing, she had a college education. I didn't know that many girls who went to college except those who wanted to be school teachers or something like that. Most of the girls in Centerville ended up getting married right after high school and having a couple of kids, although a few got jobs as secretaries. Maggie was a secretary, but she hadn't been to secretary school or anything. She worked for a lawyer, and in fact, she had gone to college to be a lawyer. The college was somewhere in New England where she had been brought up.

The story I had heard, and Will never told me this and I don't know if he knew it, was that in college Maggie had fallen in love with a guy from Centerville. After she graduated she moved to Centerville with the idea that in a year or so she and this fellow would be married. When she came to town, the only job she could get was as a secretary. After a while, Maggie and the fellow broke up, but she stayed on as secretary for the law firm to make enough money to go back to school.

"Tom, just because you love a girl doesn't automatically mean you'll get married. There are so many things that go into making a successful marriage. I haven't even thought about asking her. . . . What do you think she'd say?"

Cripes! How was I supposed to answer that? I mumbled something, but Will wasn't listening. I suppose he would have kept on talking even if I hadn't been in the room. I didn't tell Will, but I think probably she would have said "yes," although I can't see why. It was just hard to see a girl that pretty or nice with Will. Don't get me wrong. I think Will is really swell, and I don't know where I'd be without him. But he sure isn't what you'd call good looking, and the jokes he tells aren't even funny. What I'm trying to say is that it's hard to understand what girls look for in a man. Will always seemed the type that would stay a bachelor. Getting married just wasn't that important to him.

The reason I thought Maggie might marry Will if he asked her was the way she looked at him sometimes. Toward the end of last baseball season when he had her helping out at the park, she'd be in the office, and I'd be there too, counting the ticket money. Will would be doing something, like talking to a fan who didn't like something or worrying about the hot dogs being cooked enough, and she'd be looking at him with this quiet little smile on her face. He wouldn't even know it. Then she'd see me looking at her looking at Will, and she'd give me this wink like we had a big secret between us. Right then I should have figured Will was in for some trouble, and I probably should have told him. Except I kind of liked Maggie, and if she wanted to have this silly smile on her face about Will who was I to tell anybody?

Maggie's working at the park was another thing. Will had always said that he didn't like the girls he dated coming to the park. He said it distracted him, that this was his business and you shouldn't mix business with pleasure. But then in mid-season one of our ticket sellers quit and who should takeover on a temporary basis until Will could find somebody else but Maggie. She wouldn't work for money, but she was real quick at picking up selling the tickets. When I checked her in at the end of the sixth inning, she was never over a dollar off. And she'd sit in the chair beside the desk where I worked with a grin on her face as if it were some sort of joke to have me check her in. When I'd finish she would ask me real serious if everything was correct, except I knew she wasn't serious. At first it really griped me, this girl not taking her ticket selling with a good attitude. But after a while I got to like her sitting there, and I'd always check her in last so she wouldn't have to rush off after her tickets were finished.

Maggie was smart about Will, and she took the attitude that only two people really knew him, and we ought to stick together. She'd come in laughing, telling me something Will had done, and some people might have thought it strange for a girl to snicker at someone she was dating. But the things she laughed at were really funny, and I had to chuckle at them too.

It was around ten o'clock when I started getting ready for bed. Will was in the kitchen fixing himself a sandwich. He'd wound down from his Maggie talk when he called to me in the bedroom. "How was your day?"

"Not bad."

"Did those detectives stop by the school?"

"Yeah."

"They were by the ball park earlier and said they needed to talk to you. What they want?"

"Not much. Just a few questions."

"Oh, by the way. I also had a call from your principal."

Uh oh. "Yeah?"

"Little problem?"

"Little."

"Don't let it happen again. OK?"

"Sure, Will." I had hoped Will might not find out, but he knew about the bad too. I just hoped Donald didn't give me the finger in class anymore.

"Thomas! Go to the principal's office this minute!"

"Yes, ma'am."

"And class. I want you to stop that snickering. You, Donald Perkins. I've got a good mind to send you also."

The thing was it had been Donald's fault. He was the one who should have been sent. But no. I was caught. Things work out that way sometimes. And I don't think anybody in the class had been paying attention to Miss Harrell anyway. Nobody cared that Vitamin P was found in paprika, and she had been going on most of the period on that vitamin mess. Miss Harrell's got to be the most boring teacher ever created.

It was getting to the end of the sixth period when Donald started giving me the finger while Miss Harrell was writing on the blackboard. Well, if there's one thing Donald can do it's give the finger. He usually breaks up the class when he does it, and he's really practiced. There's an art to giving the finger just right. Of course, you can give it like a girl would do, just bunching up your fist and then extending the middle finger, but the way Donald does it has real style.

Miss Harrell was drawing a chart on the blackboard when Donald gave me the finger, and I had to give him one back. We kept going on for three or four minutes, and really, the whole class was enjoying it a lot more than vitamins. If it hadn't been for Steve Samson, I'd have been all right. He whispered something to me while I was giving Donald the finger, and I turned around to find out what he was saying. The only trouble was that I didn't put my finger down, and at the same time old lady Harrell turned around, and I was caught. There wasn't anything I could say, and I just picked up my books and went down to the bench. Everybody was laughing, particularly Donald, which really griped me. It should have been him.

The worst thing about going to the principal's office was sitting on the bench. Oh sure, sometimes he might paddle you, but before you went into his office, you had to sit on the bench right out in the main hall. There everybody could see you, and who likes to have people walking by and laughing as you sit and worry about what's going to happen to you inside the office. I was sitting there, worrying, hoping nobody I knew would come by, when one of the pages came out of the secretary's office. Pages are the school goody-goodys who get to work in the office during study hall. They generally make me sick. The page looked surprised to see me, and he told me he was on his way to Miss Harrell's class to get me because some men were in the office waiting to see me.

I didn't know what to think, and inside the principal's office, two city detectives were waiting to ask me questions. The principal left the office so the two men could talk to me, and the only thing I could think was maybe the principal wouldn't find out about me giving the finger. The detectives wanted to find out about my father, and I tried to tell them as best I could remember.

The thing was I didn't really remember too much about my father. Before my father left when I was five, I could remember it wasn't too good a time, and sometimes he would make my mother cry. My father drank a lot then, and I think he would hit my mother, so when he left us, everything was better. Oh, not in terms of money—it was shortly after that we had to move in with my grandmother—but I remember things were much more peaceful after he left.

From what I could tell, my mother loved my father at one time, but after he left, she never talked about him. We had no letters or calls from him, but occasionally we would get some bits of information. I think he spent a little time in jail in Atlanta, and I heard at one of our family reunions that he was involved with moonshine whiskey. Certainly, on my mother's side nobody ever thought much of him, and I guess they were glad he left. When I moved in with Will, I'd ask about my father sometimes, and Will was about the only person in the family who could say anything good about him.

"Hey, Will, what was my father like?"

"Not such a bad fellow, Tom, before he started drinking."

"Whatcha mean?"

"Oh, when he was younger, Tom, he was some talker. Fancy dresser, big car. I know when I was young and he started dating your mother, I was always glad when he came over to the house. He'd take me for a ride in his big car and usually buy me something at the candy store. Nobody was really sure what he did for a living then, and that's why your grandmother never liked him. But he sure swept your mother off her feet. He always said he was a salesman. But then things went bad with whatever business he was in, and shortly after you were born, he started drinking. He was pretty mean when he was drinking."

But the detectives didn't care that much about what I remembered of my father when I was five. They really wanted to know about the last time I'd seen him. After he left us, I didn't see him for eight years, but then he showed up last summer. It was during the baseball season, and one game I saw a man looking at me from the grandstand, just staring. I couldn't place him, but I was sure I knew him. It never entered my mind that it was my father. But I couldn't get his face out of my mind. He didn't stay at the game, because I wanted to ask Will who he was, but when I brought Will out to ask who he was, the man was gone. The next day, however, Will called me at home to come out to the park. I usually didn't come out to the park during the summer until the early afternoon, but I rode my bike over that morning and sitting in the office with Will was the man I had seen the night before.

Will was very serious as he introduced the man to me. "Tom, I want you to meet your father."

Well, my breath left me like someone had just hit me in the stomach. I'd never thought about the man being my father, but this big man stood up and shook my hand. It's hard for me even to remember what he looked like, but I was shaking hands with my own father. I didn't know what to say, but my father started talking.

"Boy, I know it's been a long time, but I think a son should get to know something about his old man. I've told your uncle here I don't want to disturb any arrangements you've got living with him. And I know being away all this time, I got no call on you. But I have to be in town this week on business, and I just couldn't let it go without seeing my own boy. I hope you won't mind if I spend a little time with you."

I looked over at Will, but he didn't say anything. I'd always wanted to get to know my father, and there wasn't anything I could say but "yes." My father told me he'd have to be leaving that morning for a business appointment, but later on in the week he'd be in contact with me.

The detectives were really interested when I told them all this, but there just wasn't that much more. I guess later in the week I saw him three or four more times, but then he was gone. He didn't say goodbye or anything, but I really didn't think that was so strange. He didn't tell anyone he was coming, and he didn't tell anyone he was going. I didn't tell the detectives this, but I didn't like my father all that much. Sure, I know a son is supposed to like his father, but most of the times I saw him that week he'd been drinking, and he just wasn't that friendly. I was happy that he'd gone, and I didn't need to worry about him.

The detectives asked me if I'd seen him with anybody that week, but he was always alone when he came out to the park to see me or took me to the drugstore for a Coke. And they asked me if he talked about anybody being after him or if he seemed scared, but I sure couldn't remember anything like that. He mostly talked about the money he was going to be making soon and asking me if I wanted to come along. But I told my father I'd just as soon stay with Will.

They must have talked to me for twenty minutes, and I answered all their questions as best I could. But what was really running through my mind the whole time was maybe I could get off without the principal knowing I had been sitting on the bench for giving the finger. Last period had already started, and when the detectives finished with me, I was going to slip up to my class and no one would ever know. But I didn't make it. It must have been that stupid page, because as the detectives left and I started to head for the classroom, the principal stopped me and told me I'd have to come back after school and stay for detention. Boy, that really made me mad. Here I'd been answering all those questions. And then the principal must have called Will. Sometimes, things don't work out like you'd like them.

5

The woman thinks it strange that you have no specific date you would like to see. "Anytime in the summer of that year," you tell her, and she leaves her desk and leads you back to a microfilm machine. Why is it that librarians are so precise, and she instructs you on which way to turn the handle so the pictures of the old newspapers will go forward. She leaves, and you turn the machine as she told you, and the old images reappear, bringing back memories that were not so far away.

It is the old box scores that you look at, the names and abbreviations of people that were so important in your life. You cheered and yelled for them, followed their every movement through these little symbols in the newspaper. They were part of your life for only those few months of a season, but their names come back immediately, and you can recite the averages, the heights, the plays. But why were they so important, why was it so easy to remember the activities of men whose actions were only meant to entertain? And the months, years, that you spent over the books, trying to memorize the battles, the leaders, the nations that shaped history are gone, never fully learned, never meant to be remembered.

There is a picture in the paper, and the team is standing in place, looking out at the camera, looking with determination. But why were they determined, why did they want to win a phantom pennant in an obscure league for a town that none of them called home? Why did you care about them, follow them? Why did they spend their manhood chasing after a white ball, and why did you spend the days of your youth following their exploits? But what else was there?

And then you see the face, the outfielder who was somehow involved. But how? And you ask the librarian for another reel so that more memories might come back to you.

"H EY,Will." I was pouring more syrup on my pancakes as Will started to clear the table.

"Yeah?"

"Did you have anything special you needed me to do at the park today?"

"Thought you might give the clubhouse a sweep." That meant he wanted me to hose it down and really scrub it.

"Mind if I skip it this morning and maybe do it later?"

"I guess that's OK. Why?"

"Oh, thought I might try to fly a kite. . . . Say, these pancakes aren't that bad."

"Thanks."

They weren't that good, either, but at least they weren't burnt on the bottom. It was Saturday, and Will would usually try to give me something besides cold cereal on weekends. Except when he cooked pancakes the frying pan was always too hot, and the last batches were always black on the bottom. Of course, I wouldn't say anything to Will, because he'd suggest I do it, and like I said, they weren't that bad.

I finished reading the paper and helped Will dry the dishes. I then rode my bicycle over to Hite's Grocery Store. They had just gotten in the kites for spring, and I picked up one. Mr. Hite had some fancy box kites and some other new types, but all I wanted was one of the 15¢ High Fliers. I couldn't see much sense in those expensive ones when the cheap kites flew a lot better. Besides, I needed a couple of rolls of string, and I didn't have that much money to waste on special kites.

When I got back from the store, Will hadn't left for the ball park yet. I decided to ride over with him and fly the kite at the ball park. Centerville Stadium wasn't the best place in the world to fly a kite, but it wasn't the worst. The light towers were the problem. Any change in wind direction could result in a lost kite. Still, if I worked it right there was plenty of clear space, and I really wanted to fly the kite by myself rather than over at the school yard where there would be a lot of other people. Nobody else would be on the field, and it was peaceful to be by myself and watch the kite as it sailed in the air.

Out at the park the wind wasn't good for flying kites, and I had a hard time getting the kite above the level of the stadium roof. When it reached that height, the wind would pick up, and I had to pull it back down twice to put on more tail. It must have been fifteen minutes before it went up permanently, and I was slowly letting out the cord as the kite sailed evenly between the light towers. I don't guess there's anything more peaceful than flying a kite when the wind isn't too strong and you can just gently pull on the string to keep the tension right. The kite was floating softly as I tied the second roll of string to the end and just looked up at the blue and white of the sky.

The wind shifted, and the kite was soon flying over the out-field fence. The city had completed putting in the new fence a few days before, and it was all fresh and bare with new pieces of plywood that Will would have painted over with advertisements. Monty was still working on his owl, wiring the eyes and the horn for its voice, and he said it would be ready by the opening game of the season.

It was funny, but I never much thought about the fence and the body. Oh sure, the first couple of days after the body was found I thought about it, and then when someone like the detectives reminded me, but mostly it was as if it never happened. It had now been two months since Millard was climbing on the fence and it fell down, pulling up the body, and from everything I heard, it would probably remain an unsolved case. No one was pushing the investigation, and there was no reason to. No one had come forth to claim the body, and finally Will had shelled out some money to have my father buried in a local plot. The local police had found no leads in their investigations.

*　＊　＊

By the time the kite had reached the end of the second string, I wasn't thinking about much of anything. I was playing gently with the end, pulling it up and down, when huge, hairy arms reached around my body and started squeezing. I was being lifted off the ground. I don't know if I was more scared at being grabbed or that my kite might get away. Then I heard a laughing voice behind me, and I couldn't have been happier.

In this world there are many types of people. One comes around behind you and grabs you and lifts you in the air and laughs. It was Boris, Boris Sullivan, and as he dropped me to the ground, I was still holding desperately to my kite with one hand as I grabbed his hand with my free hand and shook. Gosh, it was good to see Boris.

For those who are Centerville Owl fans, Boris Sullivan needs no explanation. In fact, around the Carolina League Boris was something of a legend, but, of course, the Carolina League wasn't the big leagues. Basically, Boris was the right fielder for the Owls. But he was so much more. He could really throw the ball, and I'd seen him throw runners out at the plate from the deepest part of the right field. He was big and powerful and had arms like a blacksmith's. (I once read the sports editor of the *Tribune* describe them that way. I'd never really seen a black-smith's arms.) He was the finest home-run hitter the Carolina League had seen since Leo "Muscle" Shoals was hitting home runs for the Reidsville Luckies in the late forties. The fans loved him in Centerville, and they hated him on the road, because he was big and dark and always looked like he needed a shave. He'd usually ham it up on the road to make the fans hate him more. I don't guess I said this, but Boris was my favorite player.

Boris was flying my kite as we sat on the grass and talked. He was driving to spring training in Florida and had stopped off in Centerville on his way down. We kept talking, and I got to thinking about Boris. He wasn't like most ball players. In fact, he wasn't like any player, or at least, any player that I'd ever met. To begin with, he was old. Of course, I'm old to a second grader, but

Boris was old for a minor league player. He said he was twenty-nine, except he'd been playing for twelve years, and that would have made him eighteen when he started playing professionally. That's when most ball players start, but Boris didn't start until he had graduated from college. The kite was flying pretty good so I asked him about this, and he just laughed and boomed out. "Child prodigy, Tommy, child prodigy." That means he was smart as a kid and went to college early, but I don't think he went to college three or four years early.

I think Boris's age bothered him. For me it's hard to think I would ever be twenty-nine or thirty-two or however old Boris actually was. So when I started talking to Boris about age, he became much quieter, because he's usually laughing and that voice of his is always booming. Boris's voice sounds like he looks. He's muscular and hairy, and his voice is muscular and hairy if that makes sense. Well, he started talking quietly.

"Tommy, you know, I never thought I'd be this old. My mind can't accept it, and sometimes I think I'm still twenty-one with the major leagues ahead. My mind keeps telling me I can run as fast and throw as hard, but lately my body has been trying to tell my mind that it isn't so. But my mind still won't believe, so I'm playing a game I should have given up years ago."

That really shocked me. Here Boris was saying he should give up baseball. What would the Owls be without Boris in right field? "Do you mean that?"

"Ah, Tommy, of course not. I should never give it up. Why should we ever have to give up something we love?" Boris talked that way sometimes. He was really sentimental. One time we brought some kids over from the cerebral palsy school to see a game, and Boris really took some time with them. He went around and talked to all of them and gave them these little plastic baseballs we had there to give away, but I saw him once or twice that day look like he wanted to cry.

And you wouldn't believe him with Millard. I was nice to Millard and everything, mainly because Will said I should be. But Boris acted like he enjoyed having Millard around. When

Millard was the bat boy, Boris always told him what a good job he was doing picking up the bats, and he'd play catch with Millard before the games. I think Boris protected Millard from some of the other players because they wanted Millard around even less that I did sometimes. When you're retarded, or whatever Millard is, it sometimes makes people uncomfortable, and ball players are just like other people, at least in some ways.

Boris's age didn't make him that much different from a few of the other players in the Carolina League, because the league had always had some old players. Lately, however, the major league clubs had been sending in much younger players, and only a few of the old ones were left. Jack Taylor was with the Hi-Toms and Jack Swift had been with Winston-Salem the year before, but the big league clubs now wanted their good, young players on the teams.

The thing that made Boris different from a lot of the other players was that he was kind of smart. Now, I'm not saying ball players are dumb, although I've known a couple I would have sworn were taking stupid pills. But, by and large, I guess they were like any other group of men, although most of the ones we had on the team had never been to college. But Boris had been to college up north, and he even read books. I can't remember ever seeing another ball player with a book, unless it was one of those paperback types I wasn't supposed to read. I once asked Boris what he had studied to be in college, because nobody goes to college to be a Centerville Owl. Boris told me he hadn't studied to be anything, but his specialty was political science which the way I understand it is the same as ninth-grade civics, only a little harder. He'd sometimes go to the library during the day while most of the other players would be going to movies or just standing around on the square looking at girls and making comments.

Boris started asking me questions on school and what I'd been taking. Sometimes the way he acted, I honestly believed he wanted to be a teacher when he finished playing ball. He was all the time quizzing me on things, and some of his lessons may have gotten me into trouble. I wouldn't know until the ninth grade, but I was already starting to sweat it. Boris could get you excited about things that a teacher would put you to sleep over, and it was the end of last season that Boris had said something that sounded like a foreign language. It turned out it was Latin. All of a sudden he started giving examples of how many of our words come from Latin, and then he asked me if I were taking Latin. Well, they don't give Latin for eighth graders, but Boris said that was one thing I should take. Except that in our school all the real smart kids take Latin in the ninth grade and everybody else is in chorus or shop. So at the end of February, I had signed up for Latin when teachers were taking down proposed course schedules for the ninth grade. You should have heard Monty and Donald laugh, and then the guidance counselor called me in and wanted to make sure I hadn't made a mistake in signing up for Latin. She said my English grades hadn't been that good, and although she couldn't tell me what to take, she said she wouldn't recommend my taking Latin. Well, like an idiot, I said I wanted to take it anyway, and now I had that to look forward to in the ninth grade along with algebra and some other hard subjects. I could just see me never getting out of the house for studying. When I told Boris I had signed up for Latin, he seemed pleased. "You'll do great, Tommy, great. Just don't get behind and study hard." Somehow I always managed to get behind in my subjects, and that's because I wasn't studying hard enough.

Boris was bringing in the kite when he looked out toward the fence and saw the new plywood. "What's going on out there, Tommy?" He was frowning as he stared.

"Oh, I forgot to tell you, Boris. The fence fell down and they found a body."

"Oh?"

"Yeah. It happened in January. The body had been there a long time. They said it was my father."

Boris looked at me strangely, and I don't know what he was thinking. I guess maybe he was worried about it being my father,

68

but he knew I didn't know my father that well. He kept asking questions. "How do you feel about all that?"

"Well, it was sort of scary when they found the body. I was there. And I guess I don't like to go behind the fence that much. But I try not to think about it, and I didn't know my father that well, so that doesn't matter."

"Do they know who did it?"

"Naw. The police have been out here a lot, but they don't know so much. They found a piece of pipe with the body they say was the murder weapon. It had been used to fracture his skull, but that's about all they can say. I guess they're about to close the investigation."

"Why's that, Tommy?"

"Oh, I think Councilman Waller wants them to close it. He says they've been spending too much time on it, and it doesn't help the ball club to have people remembering there was a murder out here. The police chief and the councilman are good friends, so unless something new comes up, it doesn't look like they'll ever find out anything more."

Boris shook his head. "Well, I guess that's best, don't you think, Tommy?" I agreed.

The kite was almost in and dipping up and down. I ran out to catch it before it slammed into the ground, and Boris wound up the last of the string. I tore off the tail, and we started for the office. Boris was taking me to get a "pop." You could always tell people from the north. They said things like "pop" instead of "soft drink."

Under the grandstand we stopped in the office. Boris hadn't come by Centerville to help me fly a kite, but he had wanted to see Will. Seeing me flying a kite had sidetracked him, and now he said he was going to ask Will out to supper. That seemed like an easy thing to do except Miss Elmira was in the office cleaning, and when she saw Boris she lit right into him.

"Now, where's that ball you promised? You said you was goin' to give me a ball with yo' name on it. Where is it?"

"Elmira, my all time favorite fan. Great to see you."

"Now don' you sweet talk me. You promised me a ball and I ain't seen it yet."

With Elmira standing there blocking Boris's way to Will's desk, he might never have gotten by if Will hadn't reached in the desk and pulled out a ball. He threw it to the outfielder with a pen, and Boris signed it and gave it to Miss Elmira. Normally, Will was real tight with giving anybody baseballs, except he'd do anything to keep Miss Elmira happy. Well, Elmira was happy, and she was beaming and asking Boris questions about how many home runs he was going to hit this year, and why didn't he hit more last year, and just things all fans ask. It looked like Boris would never get to see Will, so he just yelled over that he'd stop by later but now was taking me out for a Coke.

As we walked outside, a car drove up, and it was Maggie. When she saw Boris she gave a yell and rushed up and hugged his neck. Maggie was big on hugging. Well, Boris hugged right back and then took her by the arm and started leading her to the office. "Margaret, I do believe you get more lovely all the time."

Maggie just laughed and punched Boris in the stomach. Boris knocked on the front door of the office and then opened it and yelled in. "Will, I found this strange woman wandering around outside. See if you can't do something with her. I'll see you both later on."

I had been standing around watching all of this as Boris returned and we started for the shopping center. I got to thinking that you wouldn't ever see Maggie hugging any other ball players. You could never have told what might have happened if Maggie had hugged somebody like our first baseman, Hugh McDowell. Well, I think I know what might have happened, and they had laws against that sort of thing. But Maggie was smart, and she knew who she could hug, and Boris was probably the only ball player she knew at all well. He talked to her quite a bit about the things she'd studied in college and other stuff.

"Fine girl, that Maggie, fine girl." Boris was talking as we went into the drugstore. "Not what you usually find around a ball park. And I gather she and Will are still getting along well."

"Yeah. Can you keep a secret?" Boris indicated he could. "I think they might get married."

"Why, Tommy, that's tremendous. Why's it a secret?"

"I don't think Will's made up his mind, and I know he hasn't told Maggie."

"How does this affect you, Tommy?"

"Whaddya mean, Boris?"

"Well, Tom, if they get married, do you think it will do anything to your living with Will?"

Now, I hadn't really thought of that, but I couldn't see it. "Naw. Maggie and me get along fine. It won't be any trouble her living with us."

"Good man, Tommy, good man." He was laughing, but he always laughed.

That night Boris took Will and Maggie out to supper. If they had been going to the cafeteria, I might have tried to weasel an invitation, but Boris was taking them to a Greek restaurant he knew, and I don't think I would have liked the food. Boris came by to pick up Will first, and I was eating my supper. I got up anyway to say goodbye, because I wouldn't see Boris again until the start of the season. He rubbed my hair and shook my hand, and then he and Will started for the car. I heard Boris ask Will a question just as they reached the car.

"Will, what do they know about the murder?"

6

You continue to turn the handle on the microfilm machine, hoping to find something on the murder, but the newspapers forgot it as you forgot it. There is nothing, only the initial report of a body found behind a fence. But there is other news, and you wonder that it was that long ago. Sputnik was still important, and over in Winston-Salem Buddy Holley was playing a concert. Elvis Presley had just been drafted into the Army, and the advertisements push the new Edsel. On TV the "$64,000 Question," "Dragnet," and "Ozzie and Harriet" were tops.

But there seems to be an underlying theme in most of the major news stories, and you had forgotten how pervasive the question of race and segregation was. There had been the Supreme Court decisions, but the South was fighting and winning, and you wonder at how much it consumed everyone's thoughts. Was it that important in your life? Wasn't it just some-thing to be accepted, to believe it had always been that way and would remain so? But race was involved in that final summer, and it too played a part in everything that happened.

W ITH the season just three days from opening, Will was having to worry about things other than that first game. He wasn't thinking about the body anymore because the local police had officially dropped the investigation, but now he was having to worry about colored people wanting to sit in the main grandstand. Well, it hadn't really happened yet, but that's why he wasn't at the park that Saturday afternoon. You see, Councilman Waller had received some information that local leaders of the NAACP were thinking of causing a confrontation, and the ball park could be one of the places. The city had a public golf course that was segregated, and of course the city swimming pool was segregated, and the councilman was worried that the Negro leaders might pick the ball park of these three places. He had asked Will to come downtown to discuss what course of action the city and the ball club would take.

In a way Monty was caught up in the segregation thing, and it was bothering Donald and me. That's why we'd spent all day helping him finish the eyes for his owl. It looked like the owl would be ready for Opening Night, and it should have been the way Monty had been working all week. I couldn't believe how much time he took getting it wired, and he had even repainted the scoreboard numbers that week so they'd be ready for the opener.

Except I don't really believe he was working hard just because he wanted everything to be ready on time. He had been quiet all week long, and immediately after school he would leave and rush to the ball park. He acted as if he couldn't think about anything else, but I knew he was. There had been a dance on Friday, and just about everybody in our class except Monty had been invited. The dance was held at the Centerville Country

Club, and I think he wasn't asked because he was part Indian. I didn't want to go myself, but Will made me. Donald's mother pushed him, although he probably would have gone anyway, because he even goes to school dances sometimes, and nobody with good sense goes to them.

I'm not really sure why I got an invitation because I've only been out there once, but my invitation said "stag," which meant I didn't have to take a girl. If I had been given a date (all the invitations say "your date is" at the bottom), I would have gotten sick or something. Donald had a date, but it was just that skinny Vera Bell. I think the real reason I was asked is because Victoria Henderson was asking everybody in the class, or almost everybody.

The dance was held at the Centerville Country Club, which should tell you something. Victoria's father is a vice president at the mill, and you've got to have money to belong to the country club. There's one other country club in Centerville, but it isn't as good, or at least that's what everybody says. The Centerville Club has only a couple of Jews and Catholics in it.

I don't know if I really need to explain what sort of people are members of the Centerville Country Club. I guess you could call them snobs, and when they're in a group together, you might as well forget it. They'll be putting somebody down or knocking the way somebody's dressed, and you don't even need to hear what they're saying. You can tell by the way they laugh. They all dress with clothes from the same stores in town, and they talk about their Gant shirts and junk like that. I don't think I like any of them very much, except for maybe Jamey Wilson. It's surprising, but when he's off by himself, he's a pretty nice guy. He likes baseball, and because his father buys a season box seat from Will, Jamey will come out to some of the games. Monty and Donald and I have even had him hit ball with us.

The dance was bad, but I knew it would be. Everybody had on a coat and tie, and the girls were all dressed up. The boys stood on one side and the girls on the other. There were a lot of mothers standing around, all smiling and sort of pushing the boys to dance. I guess the fathers were in the bar. Liquor isn't allowed in the county, but that didn't seem to bother the country club. Some of the other stags and myself were talking about what we should do, other than dance, but the country club isn't a good place to goof around in. We were talking about stealing some toilet paper from the john and throwing it in the trees, but there's a doorman out in front, and you just got the impression that nobody in the place would think it was very funny. We did throw some sandwiches in the pool, but some of the mothers stopped us from doing that. It was a pretty dull evening. Really, Monty should have been glad he didn't get invited.

Mr. Johnson, the colored ticket taker at the ball park, was acting as a waiter that night, standing behind the punch bowl serving that ginger ale with lime sherbert they always serve at dances. I think he does a lot of things part time. Some of the rich kids were being generally snotty to him, sort of ordering him, but he would just smile and hand them the punch as if nothing was wrong.

Midway through the dance with nothing happening I went over and started talking to him. "Hi, Mr. Johnson. Lousy dance, isn't it?"

"Why, Tom. I seen you standing over there. How come you not dancing with some of the pretty girls?"

"Oh, com'on, Mr. Johnson. Most of these girls here are just drips. You've seen 'em act."

"Then why'd you come to the dance?"

"Will sort of made me. . . . Mr. Johnson, do you like all these kids?"

He just chuckled and shook his head. "Why Tom, you know they're all kinds of people in the world. You seen 'em out at the ball park. Some of these kids just actin' like their folks taught 'em. You just takes what comes."

Well, I wasn't sure if I could have taken some of the jerks who were out at the country club, but the rest of the evening me and Mr. Johnson talked baseball when he wasn't serving punch. I'm glad he was there because I'd have probably called Will to come and pick me up early, and I don't think he would have liked that. About the only good thing that happened the rest of the night was that a couple of guys got ahold of a can of beer and drank it. Some of the parents saw them, and you'd have thought the world was coming to an end. All the mothers were shaking their heads, and the boys were asked to leave, and it got pretty funny. I sort of wished I'd have found the can so I could have been asked to go and get home early.

Really, I guess Donald and I were feeling guilty Saturday when we spent the day with Monty, but he did need some help on his owl, and by early afternoon, it looked as if everything was about ready. I was getting excited, and Donald was unreal.

"Com'on Monty, let's hear the horn."

Monty just mumbled and continued working with the wires. I looked up at the huge owl, which Monty had pulled into the up position. Bright red lights now filled the eyes, and the automobile horn was perched on a ledge of the scoreboard. "Monty, this should be better than anything they ever had out here." I meant it.

"Yeah." Monty was still mumbling, but I knew he was excited. Finally, he looked down from where he had wired everything on the scoreboard. "It's ready."

He lowered the owl to the ground and stood ready on the scoreboard as he held the rope that was attached to the owl's head. With a loud whoop he jumped off the scoreboard, and the owl came to the top of the fence. And then the eyes started flashing and a loud rumble started from the horn. "Aaaaooooggggaaaahhhh!"

Donald and I were yelling and cheering, and it was really great. Only, after a while, there was a problem. It didn't stop. After fifteen seconds of the horn it began to get a little old, and the lights did not stop their flashing. I yelled to Monty, but the noise and the lights kept on. I trotted behind the fence, and Monty was rushing around checking wires. He yelled over to me. "It won't cut off."

I ran back to the front of the fence, and now smoke was coming from the eyes of the owl. It would have been a fine addition, except it wasn't supposed to be happening, and the horn was still getting louder.

And then I turned to the grandstand, and I saw this large figure walking swiftly out to us, waving his arms and shaking his fists. I couldn't hear what he was saying, but I knew it wasn't good. At a time like this, he was the last person I wanted to see. Then there was something that sounded like a small explosion, and both the lights and horn let out a small burst of fire, and then there was silence.

Monty walked out from behind the fence, and he was shaking his head. I didn't know what to say to him. I wanted to cry myself. But I didn't have a chance to do anything, for the large figure I had seen heading from the grandstand was now out near us. His voice pierced the silence. "What in the hell is going on here?"

I'd have thought after seven months or more, he might have given a more pleasant greeting, but then I don't guess I know anybody anywhere who had a more unpleasant disposition than George Fitzgerald, field manager of the Centerville Owls. Everybody calls him Fitzie or Fitz, and he'd been the Centerville manager for two years. He yelled a lot at his players, and you'd have thought we were ball players the way he was cussing at us. Everybody says he cusses out ball players as good as anybody in baseball, but they also say that when he was younger, he was much worse and always lost his temper. I can't really believe that, because it's difficult to believe anybody could be in as many bad moods as Fitzie.

He was standing beside us and had cooled down a little as I tried to explain what Monty was doing. When I finished all he could mutter was "Holy Jesus." He shook his head, turned around, and started back toward the stands. When he had gone about ten feet, he turned around and looked at me.

"Tom, you better leave your two friends with that damn owl. The team will be here late this afternoon, and I want that clubhouse straight."

79

"They aren't due until Monday."

"Wrong. They left early this morning. The bus should be in late, so get your ass in gear."

I didn't know what to think. I should have been happy, because it's always great when the team comes in town for the first time, but now Monty's owl was all wrecked. I walked over to him, but he wasn't crying. He just looked mad. I tried to say something about how I was sorry, but he just kept looking at the smoking eyes. "I'll fix it," was all he would say, and as I followed Fitzie to the clubhouse, I saw him and Donald climbing on top of the scoreboard.

"Goddamn. I hope you learned how to polish shoes this year. You were about as worthless as tits on a boar hog last year." Fitzie was arranging his stuff in the manager's office as I started pulling out the uniforms for the team. He was right. I wasn't that good at polishing shoes. Of course, it wasn't my favorite job. But then who could get their jollies out of putting shoe polish on a bunch of smelly baseball spikes. But it was the only way I made money during the summer. The ball players tipped for it, and so I'd spend an hour and a half each day doing the shoes and cleaning up the clubhouse. I didn't get paid for doing Will's tickets, because the ball club really couldn't afford it.

Some people thought from the way Fitzie talked that he was one of the most unpleasant individuals in the entire world. The truth was that although maybe I was a little afraid of him, in most ways he was all right. I know he yelled at me so I would do the clubhouse job right. He had this idea of what the clubbie should do, and I had to live up to it. They say one reason he had such an unpleasant disposition was that he had ulcers. I saw him all the time drinking this white medicine to settle his stomach. And Will even liked Fitzie. I know they'd be in the office after a game sometimes, talking a long time. Will would always try to get what Fitzie wanted for the team, providing it didn't cost too much. He always talked about how he respected Fitzie. That meant that although he thought a lot of Fitzie, they weren't really close friends.

I don't know if Fitzie had many friends. Sometimes, he knew some of the old scouts who came into town, and he was once a teammate of Mr. Carmody, the farm director. But he didn't seem that close to anybody. Fitzie's wife had been dead for three or four years, and when he came to town every year, he rented a room at the Mid-Carolina Hotel and lived there. I think he ate most of his meals in the coffee shop and never did much of anything around town. His real home was in Mississippi.

Late last season when Fitzie had chewed me out for not polishing the shoes right, and I wasn't happy about it, I asked Boris about him.

"Boris, what do you think of Fitzie?"

"Good man, Tommy, good man."

"But he drinks too much, and all the time he acts like he's in a bad mood."

"So what, Tommy. He's got one of the best baseball minds around. The major league club sends him to the Centervilles and Dubuques of the world, and he teaches their kids baseball. And the big league club sends him bad players, kids with no talent, no potential, and he puts up with them, instructs them, cares about them, even though he knows they will never make the majors. And then when he has spent all this time with these players, the big league club calls him up and tells him to release the kid. Fitzie has to be the one to tell a kid that his dream is dead. That's one of the reasons he's in a bad mood and drinks.

"Tommy, Fitzie wanted to get to the big leagues, too, because he knew baseball as good as anybody in the country, knew the strategy, knew how to handle players. When he finished up his playing career, always as a minor leaguer, he knew he could get to the big leagues as a manager. But now it is twenty years later, and he is still managing in the minors. And he still knows more baseball than any of the owners or general managers could ever hope to know. But now he also knows he will not make the big leagues, and so he has to content himself with staying around Class B leagues, because he loves baseball, cannot give it up, even though he knows his own dream is dead."

"He sure doesn't act like he's very smart."

81

"Tommy, you're going on the surface. He doesn't have an education, he talks like he's got a mouthful of mush, and his grammar is bad. And that's what some of the big leagues go on. But, Tommy, you can't judge somebody till you know them. He's one of the best, and I only wish I had half his knowledge."

"Well, why doesn't he get out of baseball if he knows he isn't going to make the big leagues?"

"What else has he got? Ten years ago he might have been able to give up the game when his wife was still alive and find a normal job and settle in some town. But he still had his dream. Now his wife is gone, his daughters are grown up and gone away, and you want him to give up the only thing he has left. Com'on, Tommy. He's good for baseball, and he's good for all the players he ever had on his teams. I only wish I'd had him when I was younger and still a prospect."

It was late afternoon, and I was about finished in the club-house when I heard footsteps running in the outside passageway. It was Donald, and I figured the team must be here the way he was rushing. It wasn't that.

"Tom, there're two men here wanting to see Will."

"Aw, Donald, tell them Will's downtown. Tell them to come back later."

"Tom, they don't look like the sort you tell to come back later. Maybe you'd better come."

I walked up with Donald to the office, and there were two men waiting in front. And Donald was right. They didn't look like fans wanting to get some tickets. They were dressed in dark suits, and each had on a hat. Both looked very serious.

I cleared my throat and tried to act older than I was. "May I help you?"

"Yes, we're here to see a Mr. Will Hilton."

"He's out. Should be back soon. Can I do anything?"

"No, we'll wait."

"I can sell you tickets, if that's what you want."

"We're not here for tickets."

"Oh. Advertising?"

"No."

I was about to head back to the clubhouse when I saw Will's old Studebaker come chugging up. Will parked the car in front, and when he saw the two men he came right up to them. I didn't have a chance to say anything, but apparently they knew who he was. Both men pulled wallets out of their inside coat pockets, and I could see them flashing badges at Will. I heard one say Internal Revenue Service and the other State Bureau of Investigation, but that was all. Will took them inside the office and closed the door. I wanted to go to the outer office to see if I could hear, but I didn't get a chance. Right then the team bus drove up, and I rushed up to help them carry the equipment to the clubhouse.

"Hey, Will."

"Yeah?"

"We really got some good players this year."

"Looks that way."

"Will, what did those two men want this afternoon?"

"They were asking some questions about your father's murder."

"I thought the police were through with that."

"Some complications, Tom. Apparently, the federal and state people have uncovered some information that your father was involved with bootlegging operations throughout the southeast."

"Oh."

"They want to find out if he was tied in with a bootlegging syndicate. Last summer the authorities were putting the heat on all the operations, and apparently that's why your father showed up in town. He was trying to lie low. Now, they want to find out why he was killed."

"So what are they going to do?"

"They want to check around the park the next couple of days and go over what the local police found out."

"You gonna let 'em look around the park?"

83

"I don't have much choice."

"Yeah, I guess so. . . . Too bad about Monty's owl, wasn't it."

"Yeah, but I'm glad he's still going to try to fix it. It'll be good when he gets it ready. Say, isn't it about time you went to sleep?"

"Sure, Will. Goodnight."

"Goodnight, Tom."

7

You have finished in the library, but what have you learned? There are some memories, some names that have come back, but you are no closer. Should you leave and continue on your trip? Perhaps not. Maybe a drive through the city, maybe something will come back, something for your memory.

As you drive, you go to the old neighborhood and by the old playground, but no one is playing. You suppose the recreation department could cite their statistics on the number of youth and adult teams throughout the city and the millions of tax dollars expended for the recreation of a new and growing citizenry, but why is no one over at the playground? There used to be kids who would ride their bikes down to the park and play baseball or football, or shoot baskets on the court with the nets that have now been torn down. But no one seems to go down there *anymore, making up rules so that the ball wouldn't go in the creek, or so that out of bounds would be the two big trees, or the unspoken rule that you don't tackle too hard because someone might get hurt. And the only one who didn't obey that rule was the girl who lived up on the hill, but she stopped playing football in the seventh grade anyway, because girls didn't play football once they got in junior high. She was too rough, so everyone was just as glad she had made seventh grade. Now grass is growing where home plate was, and there is no muddy place where you used to like to be tackled so your sneakers could get dirty and never really be clean. No kids just lie in the grass or play smear the queer with the ball or go down to the creek and try to dam it up, wondering if they'll catch all those diseases their parents said they'd catch if they played in the creek. It did smell, but it was fun to dam up, and if you didn't get picked on a team, you could always be an engineer.*

But now no one plays in the old playground, although they've organized a huge spring soccer league for kids. Soccer? That was something you played with a basketball if the air had come out of it. Now the kids all have uniforms and referees and learn all the fundamentals and every rule. Then, in the spring, the only thing was baseball, a time to get your glove out of the closet and oil it up like all the big leaguers were supposed to do. And for you the best time of spring, the best time of baseball, was the night the season opened.

"T OM, quick I need some change."

I was looking out the office door when Maggie called over from the ticket booth. The people were really coming in, and I could see a long line in front of her booth. I rushed back to the little safe in the office and pulled out some nickel and dime rolls and took them to her.

"Tom you're a lifesaver." With the big crowd and general admission being 85¢, Maggie was using up all her change. She looked out at her line. "I can't believe this crowd, can you? This is the most people I've ever seen here."

"Oh, I've seen better a couple of times." I was trying to act real casual.

"Oh, come off it, Tom," and she threw an empty coin wrapper at me.

Maggie was right. We might get as many as 3500 people if the crowd kept coming in. I was walking back to the office when Mr. Horace, the park policeman, came up. He was semiretired, and about the only thing he did was work the ball games. There was never any need of a policeman at the games, but the league said we had to have one. He looked concerned. "Where's Will?"

"Out on the field with the first pitch ceremonies."

"Well, you better get somebody to the ladies' rest room. A commode's overflowing." I locked the office door and rushed down to Miss Elmira's concession stand. I'd have to take over for her there while she went to the ladies' room.

I don't guess there's anything better in the entire world than Opening Night. Will may have gotten excited about Christmas, but for me it was the opener, and from the time I woke up at six in the morning until game time, it had been just great. Normally,

I hate to get up, and Will has to come in two or three times to make sure I'm up before I really get up. I like to sleep. But this morning I just sat staring at my Baby Ben, wishing Will would hurry and wake up.

I don't think Will likes Opening Nights as much as I do, mainly because they're a lot of headaches for him. But he finally got up a little after seven, only because I made a lot of noise in the bathroom to be sure he would get out of bed. One good thing about Opening Night is that Will doesn't make me go to school that day. I'm at the ball park all day long, and you know, he really needs me because there's so much to do. But the way he was acting at breakfast, you'd have sworn it was just another day. Usually, I'll be the one who lingers over the newspaper, and he'll be rushing me to get to school. But this morning I was rushing him, and I thought he'd never get through with the paper. There was another reason I didn't want him to pay too much attention to the paper, and I hoped he would only read the sports pages.

"Tom, what's this I see about a food riot at your school?"

"Huh?"

"Here, on the local page. It says authorities are investigating a food riot at Zeb Vance Junior High."

"Oh, yeh. It was some of the seventh graders. Did you see where the Yankees lost two?"

Will turned to the sports page. Wasn't that just like the newspaper? It wasn't anything close to a riot. But I was really glad it was Opening Day so I didn't have to go to school. Principals sometimes blame things on the wrong people, even if they're involved only a little.

I don't guess there's a person alive who doesn't know how bad food is in school cafeterias. I talked with Will about it, and he said the food was always bad when he was in school. Guys at other schools in Centerville say their food is bad too. All the schools in town have the same menu, so whoever plans the lunches, plans them to be bad for all the schools. But I can't believe that any school has food quite as lousy as ours.

If you saw the woman who is in charge of our cafeteria, you'd immediately know she runs a cafeteria that puts out awful food. She's got this sour expression on her face, and she never smiles. It's hard to believe that she's married, because if she cooks anything at home like she does at school, you'd have to figure her husband would have left her years ago. Her name is Mrs. Hempstead, and she calls herself a nutritionist. Probably the food has vitamins and all that stuff in it, but how can you get any vitamins if the food is so bad nobody will eat it.

The paper might have called it a food riot, but it wasn't anything like that at all. We weren't mad, and it was really pretty funny until Mr. Trollinger, the principal, came in. I said we weren't mad, but that doesn't mean the food was good that day. In fact, whoever had planned that day's menu had managed to combine all the worst things possible in one single meal. To begin with they served breaded veal cutlets. We call them dreaded veal cutlets, and it's nothing like you might order in a restaurant. The meat is hard and stringy, and half the time a knife can't cut through it. Then on the same plate, they had collard greens. Greens are this southern food that you can put vinegar on, and look a little like spinach, and taste terrible. I assume they still taste terrible, because the last time I tasted greens was in the sixth grade, and they must serve them at least once a week in the cafeteria. Also, they had these awful boiled Irish potatoes that give you a good idea why so many people left Ireland. And for dessert was probably the school choice for all-time worst. It was butterscotch pudding that was hard as rubber on top and watery underneath.

During the lunch period from 12:15 to 12:35, which is mostly for seventh and eighth graders, I was sitting at a table with Donald and Monty and a few others. I'd tried to cut my veal cutlet, and it was stringy as usual, and I hadn't touched the potatoes or greens. I'd taken two bites of the pudding but had given up on that, and we were just sitting around when somebody on the seventh-grade side started rattling his tray. The trays were aluminum and made a lot of noise anyway. That's another reason the food tastes so bad, because there's always noise in the cafeteria. Also the steam from the dish washing machine comes out in the lunch room, and you can smell all those odors from the garbage, and it's generally a lousy place to eat. Well, some of the seventh graders don't have good sense anyway, and when one of them started rattling his tray, another took it up, and in a few minutes there was a pretty good commotion going on.

Over at our table we'd been talking about the veal cutlet, and the last thing I remember Donald saying is, "You know, this piece of meat is about as appetizing as a large dog turd." He says things like that. The next thing I see is a veal cutlet sailing through the air. I'm not saying Donald threw it, but if he didn't, he's a quick eater, because there wasn't anything on his plate. Normally, that might have been all, because some teacher would have rushed over and stopped everything. Except the teachers must have seen what was on the menu, because none of them was in the lunch room. They must have been eating sandwiches in the teachers' lounge. Well, you'd have been surprised how well that cutlet sailed, and it landed over in the seventh-grade section where they were banging the trays. Before you knew it, three or four cutlets sailed out of that section, and then the whole place broke loose.

Mrs. Hempstead was still taking money from the people in line, and I guess she was afraid to leave her cash box sitting there. She was yelling for people to stop when somebody threw an Irish potato and hit her in the mouth. She rushed out of the lunch room with cash box in hand.

I couldn't believe what was happening. Guys were putting potatoes on the end of their forks and catapulting them halfway across the room. Even the girls got into it, and I swear it's a fact, but I saw Sylvia Freedman, who's Jewish and got to be the smartest girl in the entire school, take a bunch of wet, soggy collard greens in her hands and real casual throw them over her shoulder where they landed all over another table. It was really funny. Even the maids who serve the food didn't mind, because they're colored and know how bad that food is. I saw potatoes sticking to the ceiling, and the floor was all squishy with collard greens, and nobody was really thinking much of anything except that this might be the best thing that had ever happened in the entire history of Zeb Vance Junior High when Mr. Trollinger walked in.

Right then, everything stopped as quick as it had started, and people were picking up their forks and pretending they were eating. And, if you'd looked at the plates, you might have believed it, for most of the plates were really clean and anyway the school had been having this big campaign about cleaning your plate. Except there seemed to be an entirely large amount of food all over the floor. Mrs. Hempsted was with Mr. Trollinger, and she was pointing over our way. I was thinking it was going to be worse then sitting on the bench or anything.

I guess everyone's seen those TV programs where Indians are shown to be real crafty and smart, and they'll put their ear down to the ground and tell the white man that a group of fifty horsemen is 17 miles away. Well, in this case it was Monty who saved the day, and he's only half Indian. He must have seen Mr. Trollinger coming. Before the principal had even come in the door and before I'd seen him, Monty was on the floor picking up the veal cutlets people had thrown. As Mr. Trollinger started walking our way, here's Monty throwing veal cutlets on all our plates. They say you shouldn't eat food that's been on the floor, but I was cutting that meat and eating it, and Donald was making noises like it was the tastiest thing he'd had in a long time. By the time Mr. Trollinger was at our table, we all had a piece of veal on our plates and were eating it like nothing had ever happened.

Mrs. Hempsted was right behind him, telling Mr. Trollinger she was sure she'd seen the first cutlet fly out of our area, but there we were, sitting and chewing away. Donald started to say something about the seventh-grade section, but Mr. Trollinger was really steaming and told Donald to shut up. Then he spoke real loud and told the entire lunch room to be absolutely quiet, which wasn't really necessary because nobody was saying anything by that time. He announced he was going to get to the bottom of the food throwing, and he told everybody to pick up the food off the floor and take it to the garbage area. Then as we left the lunch room he took everyone's name. He announced that disciplinary action was going to follow.

That afternoon we started getting a little worried, because all through sixth and seventh periods, Mr. Trollinger was calling people to the office, trying to find out who started it. When he called me in, I told him I didn't really know, but that it seemed like it might have started over in the seventh-grade area. I don't think he believed me, but I sure wasn't going to say it might have started in Donald's area. When he asked me if I threw anything, I guess I lied, because I told him no. I didn't really throw anything, but I did use my spoon to hit Benjy Wilson in the back of the neck with butterscotch pudding. Of course, I didn't tell Mr. Trollinger that.

Will and I arrived at the ball park at 8:30 that morning, and we started to work right away. I set up a ticket box and started selling tickets to fans who wanted to buy them early, and I helped Will answer the phone for people calling in for box seat reservations. Maggie was coming in later in the morning to help, and most of the other people who worked at the park would be in early, because there just wasn't another game like the opener.

Stewart, our concession man, came in about 9:30, and he brought two of his helpers. They were busy moving boxes and doing all the other work that's required. The delivery people started in about that time, and cases of Cracker Jacks, popcorn sacks, Coke cups, and everything else had to be unloaded. The Coca-cola people were delivering their product, and around eleven the beer vendors arrived. I always liked to see them because, for some reason, beer truck drivers were always the friendliest sort of people. I know for a fact that they weren't drinking, because one of them once told me he'd be fired on the spot if he was ever caught drinking on the job. But I guess it must have been serving all those bars where everybody was always a little happy that made the beer drivers happy, and I'd always help them unload some of the beer, which made them even happier.

92

The roll man came about noon with the hot dog buns, and you could tell from the smell that they had just finished being baked. Stewart had been busy with everything, but when he smelled those buns, he stopped and yelled out to everybody working on the field and in the stands to come on in. He pulled some of the hot dogs out of the refrigerator and started boiling them. Then he opened a couple of the packages of fresh hot dog rolls, and in about ten minutes we were having the first hot dogs of the season. I'd have sworn there were only about eight or ten people in the park, but a couple of dozen showed up for Stewart's hot dogs. Even Will came, and that's unusual, because on Opening Day he's usually so busy running around he doesn't get a chance to eat. We all sat around eating the hot dogs in fresh rolls, and I don't believe anything ever tasted so good. Maybe about August a hot dog would not be high on my list of most wanted foods, but in April when it had been seven months since I'd had a ball park hot dog, it was great.

Stewart really didn't have to receive all his food and supplies on Opening Day. He could have gotten the stuff two or three days in advance, and it wouldn't have mattered that much. But Stewart said if food couldn't be fresh on Opening Day when could it be fresh. I guess he was right. Will thought Stewart was one of the best concession men in the business. He worked somewhere else in town, but he took running the concession stand as his most important job, and our food was good.

Although Stewart didn't know it, for me his most important job was to make the smell of Centerville Stadium right. When Stewart started cooking the popcorn that morning, my nose knew Opening Day was here. The ball park had only a small popcorn popper, and there was no way it could handle the two or three thousand people we hoped for at that first game. So Stewart started popping the kernals around ten in the morning, and all day long the thick white kernals were bursting over the sides of the revolving popping plate. They were quickly boxed and another load was started. As this process went on, the smell drifted down the concourse, into the office, and all over the park. It was the buttery, oily, salty smell of freshly popped popcorn. Every time I passed the concession stand, I would stop in and grab another handful, and Stewart didn't mind a bit, because that was part of working at the ball park, being able to get free handfuls of popcorn.

Out on the field, Piedmont was working as hard as he ever worked. Opening Night was something special for Piedmont too, and he said this was his thirty-third straight. The grass had been cut, and the field was already lined. The winter rye he had planted in January was a thick green, and I don't guess anybody could have told the difference between Centerville's field and a major league diamond. Piedmont was spending most of his time on the pitcher's mound, pounding the clay to make certain it was firm and hard.

In the stands, Councilman Waller had been able to get some city labor for the day, and four men were washing off the seats and cleaning the grandstand. With this being the mayor's one time at the park during the season, he wanted it to look like the city cared about baseball. A couple of fans were at work also, tying crepe-paper streamers in the stands and putting Will's four pieces of bunting over the dugouts.

I had been helping Elmira most of the morning, not because I really wanted to but because she had told me to. I had taken the toilet paper around to all the johns and placed it in the dispensers. I was happy to see that Will had bought a little better grade. Last year, I'd have sworn he bought wax paper for toilet paper.

Ball players were coming in and out during the morning, trying on their uniforms for size in the clubhouse. Will wasn't in the office most of the morning. A shipment of baseballs hadn't come in, and he was down at the Railway Express office trying to pick them up. Maggie had taken over for him in the office, and she was giving the players addresses for rooms and taking reservations for box seats.

Opening Night was the one night of the year the Owls sold out all the box seats. People who never came the rest of the year called up demanding special seats behind home plate. Maggie

94

was as polite as she could be and managed to satisfy most of them. Mr. Johnson, the ticket taker, was also helping out during the day, selling tickets or pitching in wherever he was needed.

It was 1:30, and I was still excited and looking forward to the Opener, when all of a sudden I began feeling really bad. It wasn't from eating too much popcorn or hot dogs, but at that time, Monty and Donald walked into the ball park. School had two hours to go, and with the two of them not in class, I knew that could mean only one thing. Somebody had told on them, and they'd been expelled for throwing food. Both of them had serious expressions, and I didn't know what to think.

"What happened? You didn't get expelled, did you?" I asked.

Monty broke out laughing and Donald had to answer. "Naw. Mr. Trollinger made an announcement this morning on the PA system that everybody in the cafeteria yesterday had to write a 300-word essay on 'Proper Lunch Room Etiquette.' I think I'll write mine on the polite way to barf in your butterscotch pudding."

"Why are you here? How'd you get out of school?"

"We figured you shouldn't have all the fun while we had to sit through Miss Harrell. We both went to the school nurse after lunch and said we didn't feel well. We told her it was something we ate in the cafeteria."

"You didn't!" I wouldn't have had the nerve after yesterday. "Sure did."

I was going to ask them more, but Stewart looked out from the concession stand and saw them standing there. "Hey, you two goof-offs. Are you gonna work at the park this year or talk? Get on in here and help me box some of this popcorn." They followed Stewart into the concession stand, and I felt relieved. I could write the essay.

About the only thing that didn't fit in the ball park that day were the two investigators, one from the State Bureau of Investigation and the other from the IRS. They were dressed in dark suits, walking around and looking at everything. They were in the office, the clubhouse, and they spent some time behind the fence. They had started looking on Monday, and nobody really knew what they were looking for. It took away from the feeling of Opening Day, but by midafternoon they left. After that they never entered my mind. When the gates opened at 6:30 people were already lined up to get in, and I knew it was going to be a great night.

It was in the third inning when I looked out to Maggie's ticket booth to see whether any more people were coming in. Will was seated at his desk, counting ticket stubs so we could verify the attendance. Most of the people were in the park, and the only person at Maggie's window was a well-dressed colored man. Before I had moved to Centerville there had been separate ticket booths for white and colored, but now everybody used the same booths. I saw the man reach in his pocket as if to buy a ticket, but apparently there was some conversation, and I saw Maggie point to the office. The colored man came up and asked for the manager, and I pointed to Will.

"Excuse me, sir. I just asked the young lady in front if it would be possible for me to purchase a box seat, and she said I would have to see you."

I saw Will gulp, and he got up out of his chair. "Are you a member of one of our player's families, sir?" Will had made arrangements that if any of the families of the colored ball players were in town, they could sit in the box seats of the players' wives' sections.

"No, sir. Just a fan."

"I'm sorry, but the only thing we have available is in the colored section."

The colored man made a slight bow. "Thank you very much." He left, but he did not purchase a ticket. I could see Will was a little upset, but he didn't say anything. I did.

"You'd have thought he'd know we have a colored and a white section. I guess he's never been here before."

Will didn't say anything but mumbled something about having seen the man before. I walked out to Maggie.

"Hey, Maggie. Why didn't you tell that man there weren't any colored box seats?"

She was a little angry. "If the G.M.'s going to go along with these laws, he's going to have to do the dirty work and enforce them. That's not my job." I guess I've mentioned that Maggie was from the North.

The colored guy coming for the ticket and the two investigators were the only bad things that happened the whole day. The Opener was great. The Owls won the game, 6 to 3, and Boris hit a home run. We had over 3,200 people, the best crowd in the league. I only wished that Monty's eyes for the owl had been ready. The big crowd would have loved that. It was after midnight before Will and I made it home, and I tried to talk him out of making me go to school the next day, what with it being late and everything. But he said no and acted like a parent. Well, at least I knew I wouldn't get expelled, and I knew the next day's lunch menu didn't have veal cutlets.

8

You are driving, and then you remember the drugstore. It has come to you suddenly but long ago he told you if you ever had any questions to come ask him. Did he mean this? Would he still be alive? Would the drugstore still be there?

The drugstore. It was one of the important places in your life. It would be good to be back in your high top black sneakers that you bought at Belks and be able to walk up to the drugstore and order a cherry-Pepsi. There wasn't an occasion that did not demand going up to the shopping block and getting a 10¢ cherry-Pepsi. It was a 16-ounce cup, and they'd put a squirt of cherry syrup in the cup at no extra cost. And on really special times, or when you had extra money, you could go next door to the bakery and buy a chocolate eclair. And so you drive, almost speed, to the drugstore, for if the old man isn't there at least you can order a cherry-Pepsi and remember the good things.

"HEY, Maggie. Let's stop and get a cherry-Pepsi."

"Tom, you know what time it is? You're already late for the park, and I should be getting ready to sell tickets."

"Aw, com'on. It won't take any time."

"All right. But hurry." She drove to the side door and I jumped out. I ordered two of the large sizes, and because the lady behind the counter knew me, she gave a couple extra squirts of cherry syrup. Maggie was right. We were late, and I ran back to the car.

She was sipping on her Pepsi and driving with one hand when she spoke again. "You wouldn't be wanting to be late getting to the park today, would you?"

"Why you say that?"

"Because the detectives are there."

"Naw."

"You sure?"

"Sure, I'm sure. I just wish everyone would forget about that. The team's in first place, and here they're still worried about some murder."

I didn't say anything more, but was thinking. Maybe she was right. Maybe I didn't want to talk to the detectives. Since the IRS and SBI had come in on the investigation, they had uncovered what they thought was a big "break" in the case. They believed the murder had been committed by someone associated with the ball club. It just didn't make any sense. Besides, who on the ball club even knew my father? The "break" was the piece of pipe they'd found with the body. The local police had always said that the pipe was the murder weapon, but the state guys had discovered that the pipe came from the clubhouse. In each player's wooden locker was a piece of iron pipe about four feet long that was used to hang uniforms on. It was one of these pieces of pipe that had killed my father.

101

That's why the agents thought it had to be someone in the club, because not very many people could get into the clubhouse. Of course, there were the players, but only two sets of keys were out. One was held by Fitzie and the other by Will, which he kept in the office. I guess someone could have made a copy of the key, but the agents didn't think so. In the last few days they had been questioning all the players who were on last year's club.

I kept thinking about all this as Maggie drove me up to the ball park. We were about three or four blocks away when I saw the crowd. Really, it was Maggie who saw them first, but in front of the park a crowd of people was milling around. I didn't understand it at first, for we were way too early for any people to be waiting in line for Maggie to sell them tickets. Then I saw the signs. They were pickets, and most everyone in front was colored. Some white people watched off to one side, but back and forth in front of the park, fifty or more people paraded up and down.

To begin with I probably should explain what Maggie was doing driving me to the ball park and why I was late. Usually, I ride my J. C. Higgins bicycle, and I'm always there at least three hours ahead of time. But the reason I was late was that I'm in the boys' chorus.

I'll have to say first off that I don't sing that good. I can hold a tune, which is more than Harley Granthan does, and he's the smartest boy in my class. The reason I'm in boys' chorus is not really of my own choosing. I did choose it, but the only other choices were band and shop. In the eighth grade you take one elective course, and since I can't play an instrument, I couldn't take band. Not that I'd want to. They have these really awful uniforms of a barf green color, and they have to march in parades, and I'm always embarrassed to see them in the Thanksgiving parade they look so bad. I wouldn't take shop under any conditions. I can just see me cutting off one of my fingers. That leaves boys' chorus. Girls get to choose Home Ec instead of shop, and I'd never tell Monty or Donald this, but I think if I'd have been given the choice, I'd have taken Home Ec. With just a little teaching, I'm bound to be a better cook than Will. I don't even think he cares what he eats, but then he serves it to me. Sometimes, I look forward to the summer just so I can have hot dogs at the ball park for supper rather than his cooking.

Boys' chorus isn't that bad, mainly because they've put boys from all the junior high in that one class, and the ninth graders really know how to cut up. Our teacher is the third chorus teacher in two years, and the reason the two previous ones quit was the boys' chorus. Half the time the principal comes in during the period to make sure we're not breaking anything. Most of the guys in there don't really want to sing, and the other half can't sing. I know I've gone from a second tenor to a baritone this year, and most of the seventh graders are first tenors. It's really hard to make a good sound out of all those guys with lousy voices who don't want to be there.

How I was selected I'll never know, but because I was in boys' chorus, I am now an official participant in the Centerville 100 Year Pageant. It's really a pain. That's why Maggie had to come pick me up. We were practicing at the high school football stadium, and it's too far for me to ride my bike. I'm a member of the Centerville Historic Youth Choir, "two hundred young people lifting their voices in praise of 100 years of Centerville history." If that doesn't make someone sick, just wait until we sing. It's a combination of selected students from the high school and all the junior highs in town. At first, I thought our chorus teacher was picking those she wanted to get even with, but she picked Harley Grantham, and he's got to be the biggest brown noser in school. I know she didn't pick for voices. The girls who were selected from Zeb Vance Junior High are all excited and think it's a big deal, but that's only because they've got some high school boys in the choir.

When Maggie's car pulled to a stop in front of the stadium, she jumped out and rushed for Will's office, and I followed at full speed. The pickets made no efforts to stop us and continued marching while holding their signs. The neatly lettered placards all protested the separate seating at Centerville Stadium. Inside the office, Will was just getting off the phone.

Maggie was the first to speak. "Will, what are you going to do?"

"Well, I just finished calling the police department. We'll have a few more men assigned tonight so there won't be any trouble."

His answer did not satisfy Maggie. "No, not that. Are you going to let them sit where they want?"

"Maggie, I told them it was the policy of the Centerville Owls to have separate seating for colored and white."

"But Will, you can change that. Why don't you?"

"Com'on, Maggie. It's not my decision. You know the city is dead set against it, but it will really be up to the major league club. The lease states they can do what they want. I've been trying to reach the farm director on the phone, but I doubt he'll change anything."

I was busting to ask some questions. I had read about all the trouble in other cities, but now the NAACP was interested in the Centerville Owls? It didn't make any sense. I broke in and asked Will why they were interested in the ball club.

"Tom, I'm not sure, but I think they feel they've got some leverage here. The city has no law on the books for separate seating, and the only thing that implies segregation is the statement on the back of our tickets. 'The management reserves the right to determine seating.'"

"But why don't they work on the 100 Year Pageant? They expect close to 10,000 people for the showing of that."

"That's the school board's stadium. The school board has at least a dozen laws to keep the races apart."

"But why us?"

"Tom, I think they're very aware of what happened with the big league club last year, and with our major league club owning us, it might be easier for them to get us to integrate." Will was talking about the situation that developed with the major league club the year before. Practically all major league teams had Negro players on their rosters. Only three teams did not, and they were the Boston Red Sox, the Detroit Tigers, and Centerville's parent club. Then in the middle of the season, the NAACP started demonstrations in front of the major league stadium. Attendance fell off drastically, and the club made an agreement with the NAACP to trade for a Negro player over the winter. Three Negroes were now on the big league club, but the owner, Mr. Fleer, was very sensitive to racial problems, and there was no telling what the reaction might be if pressure were put on the Centerville club.

Maggie had been quiet while I asked my questions, but now she had some of her own. "How do you feel about it, Will?"

"Maggie, I want to run a baseball team. I don't care where anybody sits, but I don't think the team could survive if we integrated. Two years ago we lost about fifty of our regulars when we integrated the team. Can you imagine what would happen if we integrated the stands?"

"Will, you know most people would sit where they've always sat."

"Sure, but the hotheads and agitators in town would scream so loudly that half the town would feel it was morally wrong to come out and sit in an interracial grandstand."

Maggie and Will were still talking when Councilman Waller came in. Councilman Waller's sort of old fashioned on many things, and race was one of them. Maggie became silent as the councilman spoke to Will. He told Will not to let the Negroes pressure the ball club, and if necessary, he could try to get the city council to pass an ordinance making segregated seating a legal fact at Centerville Stadium. I could see Maggie really wanted to say something, and finally she could take it no longer, and she burst out. "Just what harm will it do to let the Negroes sit where they want?"

The councilman was quick to answer. "Margaret, if that was all there was to it, why no harm at all. I don't mind sitting next to a nice, clean colored person any more than you do, and I don't think most of the good citizens of this community would mind either. But that's not the point."

105

"Just what is the point?" Maggie was a little worked up.

"The point is, young lady, that we've got a system that works. It's a way of life that I don't want to see changed."

"But just look over in the Negro community. You call that working? You've got slums, you've got poor, ignorant people. This is a way of life you want to preserve?"

"Margaret, do away with all the laws dealing with segregation, all the barriers, and are you going to change that? I doubt it. Integration will only bring more problems than you can imagine."

"But you don't know it won't work. You won't even give it a chance."

"You don't know your way will work, either, and if we do away with the system we have now, we can never bring it back. Certainly, it would be beautiful to believe that the two races can live idylically in a society where everyone is equal, where everyone loves their fellow man. Unfortunately, I don't think this is possible."

"But you've got to give it a chance. You've got to see if it's possible."

"No, I don't, young lady, and as long as I am an elected official in the city of Centerville, I will do everything in my power to preserve segregation. That includes segregation in this ball park." The councilman walked out.

All this time I had been working up Maggie's tickets, and I could see she was steaming. Will had just been sitting there listening, and Maggie was shaking her head. Then she saw my ticket box and grabbed it.

"OK, Will Hilton, I'll sell your tickets tonight, but I don't like it. I don't like what's going on here, and I may not want to be associated with this organization. So when I cool down, I'll think about it and let you know what I'm going to do." And she stomped out.

I left Will in the office and went out to look at the demonstrators. I counted them, and there were thirty-seven, and all but one of them were Negroes. The one who wasn't was the Reverend

Tillman, the minister over at the Friends Meeting House. He's white, but he was always involved in the racial and "ban the bomb" stuff, and nobody was surprised he was there. Most of the demonstrators looked like college students, and all the men had on coats and ties. I'd once seen picket lines over at the textile mills when a union was trying to organize, but of course, the mill owner broke that union and the strike, and everybody was back at work in a couple of days.

The demonstrators must have done some real planning and telephoning, because press people, photographers, and even TV people were there. The pickets kept marching and occasionally singing as the fans started to come in. But it just didn't look right. What were they doing at Centerville Stadium? It was a baseball park, not a factory, not a textile mill. Why were they dressed so well? Why did they have on coats and ties? Didn't they know you don't wear a tie to a baseball game? And they had signs that were neat and well-lettered. Why would anyone take so much time for the Centerville Owls? It was just a minor league baseball team, and its seating was no different than any other minor league club in the south. Couldn't they come back another year when the Owls weren't fighting for first place? Couldn't they come back when people were ready for integration? This was the south, and it was the way things had always been done.

I went back to the office. Will was still sitting at his desk. None of this was fair to him. "What's going to happen, Will?"

"Tom, I don't know."

"Can't you just tell them to go away?"

"It's a public sidewalk. They've got a right to march."

"Have you talked to the major league club yet?"

"I just finished talking to the farm director. He told me to sit tight, and maybe they'll go away."

"You think they will?"

"No. The leader of the group made a statement to the press that they will keep marching until segregation is ended at Centerville Stadium, even if it takes a hundred years."

"That doesn't sound so good."

107

"No, it doesn't."

I left. I tried to forget about integration and everything else, and I started wandering around the park. I did that most of the games. Usually, I had to spend two or three innings working on the tickets, but the rest of my time during a game was free. For four years Centerville Stadium had been as much my home as was Will's house, and I don't guess I was any happier than when a game was on. I liked baseball, sure, and it was great to see Fitzie arguing with the umpires or Boris making a tremendous catch in the outfield. But as much as the game, I liked the people. I knew everyone who worked at the stadium and many of the fans, and each night I would be in a different part of the ball park. Some nights I might go out with Monty on the scoreboard, and at times I'd carry Donald's tray of Cokes and sell some for him. Often I'd sit with a group of fans I didn't know, but that didn't matter. We all liked the Owls.

I might stand at the front gate with Mr. Johnson, and he would tell me about his days with the railroad. He had traveled from Washington to New Orleans, and he had stories about all the famous people he'd served. And sometimes I might go and visit Miss Elmira in the colored concession stand. She'd be worrying about something and have me run up to the main concession stand because she was about to run out of this or that. That was just her way.

When I sat with Councilman Waller in the box seats, he would tell me about all the old ball players who had been with the Owls in the '20s and '30s. Sometimes, I'd even say something to Millard. He had his job as a batboy, but I'd wave at him, and he'd sort of nod at me. He was trying to act like the players, and they weren't supposed to talk to fans during the game. And there was Maggie to talk to in the office, and Stewart who gave me popcorn, and Piedmont who needed beer in the groundskeeper's room.

But I couldn't enjoy my wanderings, too much was happening, and I headed back to the office. In front, the demonstrators were still marching, but with most of the crowd in the park, many had drifted off. As I watched them, I couldn't believe it. Here came Donald. He had been up in the stands with his Cokes, but it must have been slow, for now he was out in front selling to the marchers and the press. Donald will do about anything for money.

Usually I didn't check Maggie in until after the sixth inning, but I saw Will and he said I might as well take her in at the end of the fifth. It didn't look like anyone else was coming. As soon as I took her cash box, the marchers stopped, and within ten minutes they were gone.

With Will being so low, I didn't really want to be around the office, and Maggie didn't help things by not talking to him. I finished counting the money and came back to the stands and sat high in the grandstand. One of the Owls hit a home run, and I saw Monty jump off the scoreboard. The owl came up on its hinges with lights flashing and horn blowing. That was about the best thing that had happened at Centerville Stadium, but with all the problems nobody really noticed. Monty had worked hard to make the owl look just right, and I wished more people were cheering it.

I was still watching the owl flashing his eyes when two men came up the stands toward me. I had completely forgotten. It was what had been bothering me earlier in the day. The two agents who were in town to question different people with the club were now coming to talk to me. They were wearing suits, and they seemed as out of place as the demonstrators had been outside. They sat beside me, and I started answering their questions. At first, they asked the same questions as the city detectives. They asked if I'd seen anyone strange hanging around, and they asked if my father had said anything about someone being after him. Again, I had to answer no to these questions.

Then the two men asked me about the times I'd seen my father that week, and the taller of the two asked me if I could pinpoint the last time I'd seen my father. It was funny that the city men had never asked that question, because I knew the answer to that one. I reached for my wallet and pulled out a schedule from last year's team. I tend to carry a lot of old things in my wallet, and that's why it's always so fat. I probably should clean it out. I started looking at the dates of the previous year's games.

"I think this is it, July 23rd. You see, the team was in Wilson that night, and that's the only place the team will spend the night without coming back to Centerville. My uncle went east that night too, so I remember spending time with my father." I also remembered I was all alone and sort of scared when my father called to say he wanted to see me. I didn't tell the detectives that, and they kept asking questions to make sure I was certain of the date. In a few minutes they both started back down the grandstand.

The taller of the two spoke as they were leaving. "Son, you've been a big help. You know, you may have been the last person to see your father alive." I didn't know what to say, so I didn't say anything, and I started thinking about that final night. As well as I could remember, it hadn't been good. My father was drunk, and when he drank he talked too much.

"Boy, you gotta come with me. You're showing too much of your mother's blood. Them Hiltons are too weak. Look at your uncle. He's never shown much backbone, going off to Korea with them nurses rather than fighting. Now, my side, we do what we have to do. You remember that. When you gotta do something, you do it. Don't mess around."

My father kept drinking from his beer bottle as he gave me this lecture. I didn't like it. Here he'd been in town only a week, and already things were falling apart. That's one reason Will was out of town. My father had been telling people around town that he was going to take me with him. Will had gone east to check with my mother's lawyer to see if he couldn't make himself my legal guardian. My mother had never divorced my father, and I guess maybe he did have a right to take me with him. But I sure wouldn't have gone. I know it wasn't right to say, but I didn't like my father. He was all the time talking big and saying what he was going to do, but near as I could tell, he'd never done much.

"A boy should be with his father, and I aim to take you along. You got to learn what the world is like, and it's for sure you'll never learn here. It's hard out there, and I aim to make you hard, boy. Now get off your ass and get me some more beer."

I shouldn't have been in the ball park with Will away, but my father had come by the house and told me to come with him out to the park. He wanted to get some beer, and he knew I could get the keys to get him in. He was already drunk. I knew it was wrong and Will wouldn't have liked it, but I guess I was afraid of my father, and there wasn't much I could do about it. My father drove us over, and with the park all dark and nobody there, I'd gone into the concession stand and taken out some beer for him. We sat in the stands for a while as he talked and drank a six pack, and then he wanted me to get him some more. I really didn't want to, and I really wanted to get away from him. But what could I do? I just hoped Will would understand.

When I came back, my father was trying to walk to the field and he could hardly stand up he was so drunk. But he grabbed me by the neck and shook me hard. "Boy, I'm going to make you tough. I'm going to get you away from all these niggers at this lousy stadium and all these women, and I'll make a man out of you. When I get through, you'll know what the world's about. You got my blood, and I aim to bring it out. I can't take you with me yet, but in a few weeks everything will be cooled down. I may even go to see your mother once more. And she thought she was rid of me. And then I'll come back and, boy, you be ready, 'cause there ain't no way that uncle or anybody but me can keep you. And I'll show you my business and how a man makes money. And boy, you'll be tough when I finish." And he hit me on the side of my head.

My thoughts were broken by a loud noise, and I looked up to see Monty's owl coming up on the scoreboard. The horn was blowing, and I hadn't realized it but the game was over. The Owls had won it. I walked down to the office, and Will was sitting in the office going over his postgame paper work. I didn't say anything and just sat. I figured Will didn't really want to talk with all the problems with the demonstrations, and I didn't feel much like talking either. We must have sat there for forty-five minutes without saying much of anything, and then it was time to lock up. He asked me to go down to the clubhouse to make sure everything was closed down there.

It wasn't, and inside Fitzie and Piedmont were drinking beer. I wasn't really surprised, for half the time when we closed up, the two would be in the clubhouse getting drunk. I don't think Fitzie wanted to go back to his hotel room, and Piedmont would use any excuse to get drunk.

I never did understand Fitzie and Piedmont drinking together. Fitzie was from Mississippi, and people from Mississippi didn't think about colored people the way most folks did. Sure, I knew the North and South had a little different feeling, but in Mississippi it was a lot different. I never heard this for an absolute fact, but more than a couple of people said that before Fitzie got his first colored ball player a few years back, he swore he'd never manage one. Now, he'd had colored ball players for four years, and from all accounts he treated them just like any other ball player (which wasn't too good).

I told Fitzie we were closing up, and the two followed me out of the clubhouse. Will usually gave Fitzie a ride to his hotel, and on the way Will told Fitzie about the demonstrations. Fitzie really cussed for a while, talking about "the goddamn niggers," but all of a sudden he cooled down. "Will, if you have to integrate and need some support with the major league club, I'll help anyway I can."

"Thanks, Fitz, but I talked to Carmody tonight, and he wants us to try to keep things the way they are."

We dropped the manager off at the hotel. He carried a fresh six-pack through the door.

112

9

You are heading for the drugstore, and as you round the corner you feel elation, for this is something they have not torn down. But the name is different. You park the car and walk in, and some of the same women are still working in the store. Of course, they are older, and you see one dusting the merchandise someone might buy if they were sick. But the soda fountain, the soda fountain, is gone, and you will not be able to buy a cherry-Pepsi. You suppose it had to go, it was small with only three stools, but why do they always take the good things.

The magazines are still in one corner, you used to read them for free, and they still have a small candy counter. You go up and buy a Mounds bar. The woman waits on you, and you ask about the soda fountain. She tells you it went out years ago. And then you ask about the old owner, the councilman, and she tells you *he has not owned the business for many years. But he is still alive, and although she hesitates at first, she consents to give you his phone number. You leave with your candy bar wondering if you should bother an old man you have not seen in twenty years.*

I was riding home from the stadium on my bicycle. It was early evening, and with the team on the road, I had spent the day helping Will with his concessions inventory. It was getting dark, but I didn't mind. In fact, one of the reasons I rode my bike to the park was so I could ride it home in the evenings and nights. Will could have given me a lift in the car, and when I rode over it was usually hot and muggy from the afternoon humidity. But at night it started to cool off, and there was a breeze from the bicycle, and I could smell the green summer smells of the evening.

It was easy to describe Centerville from some of the smells. If I had been blindfolded and someone had taken me out to the mill village, I would have known I was there, just from the odor of the big smokestacks and the smelly dye they dumped in the river. And colored town had its own smell too, a dusty odor, mainly because most of the streets hadn't been paved. There weren't as many trees, and the houses were wood frame and looked like they smelled dusty.

And you could tell the wealthy section, because all the vice presidents and rich people lived in that area. They had big lawns with the grass always cut, and it smelled like someone cutting grass. The country club was in that section also, and with its golf course, it added to the smell of cut grass. Downtown smelled like the Duke Power buses with exhaust fumes lingering in the air.

But the average neighborhoods like where Will and I lived in Centerville smelled green. That's hard to explain, but in early spring everything would start coming up, the dogwoods would bloom, and until late September everything would smell like it was green and growing. It was a sweet smell. In the late evening you could walk around and just know that all over Centerville it smelled that good. People would sit out in their yards and open

115

up all the windows and let the cool breezes blow through, and I guess all the insides of houses smelled that good too, except for the rich people who had air conditioning and couldn't smell the green.

I tried to concentrate on the smells as I rode my bike, rather than think of everything that had gone on. The demonstrators were still outside the ball park, Mr. Carmody had come to town, Maggie had turned down Will's proposal, and two of the main suspects in the murder were now Will and Boris.

The proposal had happened that afternoon. It took place in the concession stand, and the only worse place I could imagine would be the men's room. I'm probably being unfair to Will, because I'm sure he didn't give much thought to where he was going to ask Maggie to marry him. He'd probably just gotten up the courage, and at that time he happened to be in the concession stand. But the really bad part was that I was there too. I mean, who wants to hear someone propose to someone else. Which is why there were about 150 other places I'd have rather been.

What brought it all on was Mr. Carmody coming into town and giving Will the raise. In many ways Will is really practical or maybe just old-fashioned, but I don't think he'd have ever asked Maggie if Mr. Carmody hadn't given him that raise. Will felt he should be earning enough money to be able to support Maggie. I personally thought it was a little stupid because he never gave it much thought about having enough money when I moved in. Besides, Maggie was working anyway.

But other than the money, the proposal sure didn't make much sense at that time. The two of them still weren't getting along as well as before the demonstrations started, and although Maggie was still selling tickets, I know it bothered her a lot. A couple of times I heard Will and her talking, and Maggie was trying to convince Will that he should open his seating. But things stayed like they were.

The main reason Mr. Carmody came to town was the demonstrations. They had now been going on for five weeks, and our attendance had been cut. The number of pickets had dropped to

116

fifteen or twenty a night, but very few of our colored fans came anymore. At best only five or six a night would show up, and these were the old fans who had been coming for years and years. White attendance also dropped, and the Owls were no longer leading the league in attendance.

Our colored employees had been affected. They had been receiving phone calls asking them to quit, but there was no way Piedmont would stop work. This was his full-time job, and he loved the park too much to let racial matters concern him. The demonstrations did bother Mr. Johnson, and a week after the pickets started, he came in to Will to quit. He had been in a railroad sleeping car porters' union, and although he didn't want to let Will down, he felt he should be on the picket line. But Will didn't want to lose Mr. Johnson. He had been with the club too long, and he really was a good gateman, knowing most fans by name. So Will and Mr. Johnson worked out a system where Mr. Johnson could take tickets and still show his support for the demonstrators. It seemed screwy to me, but Will did things like that. In the second or third inning, when the crowd stopped coming in, Mr. Johnson would leave the front gate and go pick up a sign and carry it. If a late arrival came, he would just put down the sign and take the man's ticket. I thought our regular fans wouldn't like that, but Will got very few complaints.

Miss Elmira was another matter. Nobody was going to tell her what to do. When the pickets first started, some brought food and would drop paper on the sidewalk in front. This was more than Elmira could take because she always swept out there in the afternoon. She marched out and told the demonstrators they should put their trash in a waste can and stuff like that. Miss Elmira could boss as good as anybody I ever saw. From then on I don't think I saw any trash on the sidewalk in front. But with no colored people coming to the games, there wasn't much point in having her open the colored concession stand. So Will just closed it and put Miss Elmira in the main stand. Nobody much thought anything about it, but it was the first time the concession stand had been integrated. About the only one who cared was Stewart, the concession man, who had to listen to Elmira tell him how much salt to put on the popcorn.

"Will, let me say that the major league organization is tremendously sympathetic with what you've had to go through down here. We know your attendance is going to be off, and there just isn't much you can do about it. But don't let it worry you. The team is going to stay. Centerville has always been one of our better minor league operations, and we feel that when this has blown over, the town will come back even stronger."

The day before Will proposed to Maggie, Mr. Carmody flew into town. I was working on my tickets in the front office as Will and the farm director met in the back room. One of the good things about the office was the thin walls. Normally, I don't spend that much time sitting around the office, but when something important was happening, I managed to find work to do in the front office. I knew it wasn't quite right for me to listen in, but I did it anyway.

Mr. Carmody made a couple of trips a year to Centerville anyway to look at players and generally see how things were going, but the demonstrations were the main reason he had come in this time. He was the farm director, and for those who aren't really into baseball terminology, the farm director is the guy on the major league team who's in charge of all the minor league teams. That meant he was both Will and Fitzie's boss, and of course he was the players' boss. If I'd have gotten money from Will for the work I did around the office, he'd have been my boss too. That was one good thing about Will not paying me.

Mr. Carmody had a big gut, he chewed cigars without lighting them, and he drank a lot. I know, because when he called Will to tell him he was flying in, Will had to drive up to Guilford County to buy a couple of bottles of bourbon. Centerville's dry except for beer, and the nearest county that sells hard liquor is Guilford. You can buy moonshine around Centerville, but sometimes the stuff's poisonous, and I don't think Mr. Carmody would have liked the taste.

118

Mr. Carmody was drinking the bourbon as he talked to Will. After he brought up that the Owls were going to stay in Centerville, he told Will about the raise. "Will, before I left I talked with our owner, Mr. Fleer, and he asked me to give you his personal thanks for the way things have been handled. In fact, knowing all you've been through and knowing your salary hasn't changed in the last couple of years, we've authorized a $150 a month raise effective immediately."

Will was pleased, and he thanked Mr. Carmody. But he still wanted to talk about the demonstrations. "Mr. Carmody, what happens if things don't cool down and the pickets continue?"

"Oh, Will, I wouldn't worry. We think they'll get tired and quit shortly. But if they do continue and you think some change is needed in your position, go right ahead and make it. As I've said all along, we have complete confidence in your judgment in these matters, and we'll go along with whatever you think best."

The two continued talking, but I decided to leave the office. I walked out into the stands and thought about what I had heard. It was good to see the big league club liked what Will was doing, and I wondered what he was going to do with all that money. I guess he must have been thinking the same thing himself, because the next day was when he talked to Maggie during the concession inventory.

It was a Saturday, and that was one reason Maggie was at the park during the day. The team was going out of town for a couple of days, and Will decided it would be a good time to get to the concession inventory. Mr. Carmody was still in town that day, waiting for a late afternoon plane, and while we did the inventory he was in the office giving an interview to Joe Ingram, the sports editor of the paper.

To begin with, doing a concession inventory is not a swell job. If you like counting popcorn boxes and paper cups, you might consider it OK, but I can think of a lot of better things. I was up in the loft over the main stand where all the boxes are stored, counting the Cracker Jacks. Maggie had just crawled up with me to see how many cigarette packs were left. Don't ask me why

Will wasn't doing any of the lousy part, but he was just standing at a table writing down the figures we told him. I'm not sure how Maggie got into the act, but Stewart couldn't be there, because it was Will's job to count everything once a month to see if the concession man was doing what he should be. Once the count had been made, I had to help Will balance everything, doing most of the math and paper work.

If I hadn't been in the loft when Will started to ask Maggie to marry him, I could have left. I sure wanted to, but Maggie was between me and the ladder, and there was no other way down. And Will was down there, stammering, and playing with the pencil as his face got all red. I was squirming around, wishing I could be someplace else.

At first, I think Maggie was just eating it all up. She just grinned over at me, and I didn't know what I was supposed to do. She was at the top of the ladder as Will kept on talking. I probably should repeat the proposal as best as I can remember, for it's nothing you'd ever hear. Maggie had finished yelling down a cigarette count, and Will was fiddling around with a piece of paper and a pencil.

"Twenty-three Old Golds? OK. Hey, uhh, Maggie, you know Mr. Carmody came in yesterday, and he, uh, said he was going to give me a raise. I'll be making a little more money which means we could have more, and I was wondering if you would get married?"

Now doesn't that take the cake for asking somebody to get married? I was about to yell down "forty-seven Cracker Jacks," but when he said that, it stopped me cold. I wanted to get out of there quick, but Maggie was between me and the ladder, and there was no other way down.

Maggie was grinning at everybody being uncomfortable, and she finally spoke, putting on this little girl southern accent. "Why, Will Hilton, you do just sweep a girl right off her feet." I guess that must have woken Will up to the fact that a concession stand on a hot Saturday afternoon might not be the best place to propose, and he became apologetic.

"Maggie, I'm sorry. I'd just been thinking about it, and with the money I thought I could ask you."

Maggie stopped smiling after a while. She was no longer kidding around. She and Will were staring directly at each other. I guess they'd sort of forgotten me. "What's the money got to do with it, Will?"

"Well, now we can afford to get married."

"Don't you think some things other than money ought to be considered or at least be brought up when two people talk about marriage?"

"Sure. What, Maggie?"

She waved her hand around the concession stand. "This, and love, and a lot of other things of which money seems to me to be about the least important." She stopped, looked at her Old Golds, and then started again. "I've thought about it, Will, but everything we do is built around this ball park. This is the only time I see you and about the only thing you ever think of. Look at the demonstrations. You don't think in terms of right or wrong, just what they will do to your ball club. Can't you see how they make me feel?

"I don't know, Will. Do I want this for a life? Your whole basis for asking me now seems to be that the ball club can pay you enough so we can get married. Somehow, I'd like to think I was the main reason you wanted to get married, not your salary."

Nobody was saying anything. I didn't know if they were going to argue, or what, but I did know I had to get out. I cleared my throat, pushed Maggie out of the way, and climbed down. I said something to the effect that I'd be in the office and left the two of them there, still looking at each other.

It wasn't two minutes before I heard the door to the concession slam and saw Maggie rushing to her car. I was in the office then, and I probably should have gone back to help Will with the inventory. But I couldn't. I had gone to the office to get away from the marriage proposal, and now, sitting there, I was hearing things I didn't like at all. Joe Ingram, the sports editor, was interviewing Mr. Carmody.

121

"Mr. Carmody, any thought on the major league level that the racial problems might cause you to move your farm club?"

"Joe, we hope not. We've been getting inquiries and a bit of pressure from some Negro groups, but the town has been too good a franchise for us to foresake it when one controversial situation arises."

"What about desegregating the stands?"

"Joe, we feel that decisions that affect the local operation should be made on the local level. We've complete confidence in the ability of our general manager to handle this situation, and we're confident that Will's decisions will be in the best interest of both the major and minor league club."

"What's the future of the Owls?"

"Of course, we want to put a pennant winner in here for Centerville, but also we want to put on a show of support for the local club to forestall those rumors that we might consider moving the club. I realize the city doesn't have much money to spend on the stadium, so in the off season we're going to spend some money on this park. You can quote me on that."

I heard Mr. Carmody clear his throat, and he started talking again. "Joe, you've been asking the questions, and now I need to ask a few myself. What are these rumors I keep hearing that a murder is connected with the ball club?"

"It looks that way. You know that body found last winter turned out to be the kid's father. Well, state and federal people became involved when it looked like it might be tied in with an illegal liquor syndicate. Now, they don't think so. This is confidential, but I was talking with our police reporter, and the two main suspects now are your G.M. and the right fielder."

"Boris? Will? I can't believe it."

"It's true. The only two who can't be placed on the night of the murder are Will and Boris."

"How do they know what night the murder took place?"

"Apparently, the last person to see the man alive was his son. The boy pinpointed the date."

"Tom?"

"Yeah. Seems like they were in the ball park together one night, and the boy told the investigators his father was pretty drunk. Nobody saw the man after that."

"Why would Will or Boris want to commit murder?"

"Well, the father was spouting off around town how he was going to take his boy with him. He was a pretty shady character, and Will might have wanted to protect the boy."

"Will had no alibi?"

"He says he was out of town, and a lawyer in Goldsboro did meet with him at 10:00 the next morning. But according to police, he could have left late that night to make the drive east and been there in plenty of time for a meeting."

"And Boris?"

"The team was playing out of town that night, but Boris didn't play. The investigators looked over the box score from that game, and then talked with Fitz. Boris wasn't with the team that night. He had an impacted wisdom tooth, and Fitzie had called from Wilson for an appointment in Centerville the next morning for Boris. Boris apparently caught a ride back to Centerville early that evening. And, what is more damaging, Fitzie had given Boris the keys to the clubhouse so he could leave his uniform off."

"But why would Boris want to kill the father?"

"He's pretty close to Will and the kid. You never can tell."

"Well, I just can't go along with any of this. Here the big league club is trying to develop ball players, and all I keep hearing 500 miles away is about demonstrations and murders. I'm ready for things to settle down here."

"Our police reporter is betting the case will remain unsolved. He thinks the federal and state people are about to turn it back to the local authorities unless they get some new leads that tie the murder back to the bootleggers."

"Well, I hope this thing is over soon."

I heard some shuffling of chairs, and the farm director spoke again. "Joe, I think it's time I should be getting to the airport. Could you give me a ride?"

123

"Sure."

"Let me say goodbye to Will and Fitz, and I'll be right with you."

Mr. Carmody walked by me through the office, and he was followed by Joe Ingram. I sat, not knowing what to think. Everyone knew there was no way Will could hurt anybody, much less kill my father, and here he was a suspect in the case. It was just stupid, and I felt very empty inside. And how could Boris have killed my father? They were wrong, all wrong.

I looked out and saw Mr. Carmody getting in the car with Joe Ingram, and I made my way back to the concession stand. I wanted to say something about what I had heard, but Will didn't look so happy. I guessed things hadn't ended up so well with him and Maggie.

"What'd Maggie say?"

"Not much."

"She gonna marry you?"

"I don't think so. Hey, let's stop the inventory for the rest of the day. We can finish it tomorrow. I think I'll go run some errands." And Will left.

So much had happened that I had to talk to someone. I wandered around the park, and noticed that the team station wagons were parked in front. That meant the club hadn't yet left for the short trip to Thomasville, and maybe Boris was around. He was in the clubhouse, and I asked him if he had a minute. We went out and sat in the stands.

The first thing I told him was about Will and Maggie. I sort of expected Boris to be on Will's side, but he leaned toward Maggie. "You know, Tommy, she may be right."

"About what?"

"About Will and baseball."

"What do you mean?"

"I don't know if she doesn't feel she might take second place to a ball park." Boris paused and then started up again. "Did I ever tell you I was married once, Tommy?"

I had heard it somewhere, but before I answered Boris was

talking again. "I was in Santa Barbara that year, Tommy, still a prospect with a future ahead of me. She was a California girl with blonde hair and a tan, and I was this dark, hairy person from the east who loved baseball and little else. And she didn't know baseball and couldn't care about it, but we fell in love. After the season I stayed in Santa Barbara and got a job teaching school. That winter we were married. We had a place on the beach where she could walk beside the ocean, and when I came home from school each day, I would sit down with her and try to teach her everything I knew. And she was looking forward to the baseball season, looking forward to something new and exciting. When I left for spring training she was eager to follow, to come to whatever town I would be sent that year.

"But, Tommy, that was my year for the Northern League, and I was sent to Fargo, North Dakota, and when she arrived it was cold and windy, and it even snowed one day. She couldn't understand what I was doing there, why I would want to play baseball in an old and depressing park when I could be in Santa Barbara on the beach. And when the summer came, it became hot on the northern plains, and there were no ocean breezes. I was traveling to Winnipeg and Aberdeen and Duluth while she had to stay in Fargo. She didn't know anyone, didn't have any friends, and she never could understand what she was doing there. In August I sent her home early to Santa Barbara, and then I joined her in September. She could not understand my baseball, and for the first time there was tension between us as she tried to talk me out of returning to baseball. I loved the girl, and by then I knew that I would never make the big leagues. I seriously considered quitting, giving up my career and settling down with this girl. But they sent me my contract, and in March I could not stay away from baseball and I left her. I was sent to Albany that year, and I wrote for her to join me, but my letters were never answered. I finally called, but she said she wasn't coming.

"I never went back, Tommy, I never could. She never could understand how I could love a silly game as much as I loved her.

She's remarried now and has two little girls, and it tears me up sometimes to think I might have had her. But I don't."

The horns were honking from the station wagons in the parking lot, and Boris had to leave. But I hadn't told him what I'd heard in the office, and as he started for the front I blurted out. "Boris, they think Will or you might have killed my father. I heard them say it."

The outfielder stopped, turned around, and smiled at me. It was a soft smile, and I don't know what he was thinking. I kept talking. "Boris, I know it's not true, but what's going to happen?"

"Tommy, first, don't worry about Will. You know he couldn't have done it. And don't worry about me. I've been able to take care of myself for a long time. But you, Tommy, what do you think about all of this?"

That was the problem. I didn't know what to think. It should have been such a great season. The team was in first place, Monty had his owl working, and everything I loved was at the ball park. But now there were the demonstrations and the murder, and things weren't like they should be. All I could answer Boris was, "I don't know. I don't know."

The horns were still honking from the station wagons, and Boris had to leave. I wanted to talk longer, but he patted me on the shoulder and ran for the parking lot. I was alone. I stayed around the ball park for a couple of hours longer, not really doing much of anything. Then with the sun starting to set, I got on my bicycle and started riding home, and as I rode I tried to concentrate on the smells, the green smells, and not think of anything else.

10

The call has been made. The old man remembers you. He seems glad to hear your voice, and for a few minutes there is the surface conversation. But you have a question, this doubt, and you tell the old man you want to find out what happened that final year. He says he thinks he can give you some answers. The old man tells you he would like to come out to the ball park, to talk with you at the stadium, for it has been years since he has visited the park. It would be good for both of you to come to the place where you always knew each other. You agree.

You hang up and wonder if you really want to know. Would it not have been better to let things dead rest? Is it not better to have some questions unanswered? But it is too late now, you have made the move, and you start your drive to the place that at one time was the most important location for you in the entire world.

THE Owls forfeited a game, and it was all because of me. It isn't good to lose a game because everybody leaves the field, but sometimes there are more important things. Not that the Durham Bulls really wanted to win by forfeit, but when the Owls came to help Will, it was automatic. It's a league rule that any player leaving the field to go into the stands or in this case under the stands is ejected from the game.

It started out like any other night . . . well, like any other night since the pickets had started. Our crowds were still down, but most of the regulars really didn't notice the demonstrators anymore. In the third inning, Mr. Johnson had picked up one of the signs and joined the pickets marching back and forth in front of the gate. In the next two innings, only six people showed up, and he put down his sign, took their tickets, gave his usual pleasant greeting, and then went back to picketing.

I was beginning to know most of the protesters by name because when we'd open the gates in the seventh inning most of them would come in and buy a hot dog and a drink. Not many of them were baseball fans, only a few stayed to watch the games, but Will didn't mind them coming in to buy sodas. He was looking for every dime he could get for the ball club. That night there were a dozen people other than Mr. Johnson picketing. None of the leaders of the NAACP were doing much marching anymore, and on this Thursday night, there were eleven colored college students and the Reverend Tillman, the Quaker minister.

The way things were going it looked like it was going to be a stalemate. Councilman Waller had a proposition ready to present to the City Council to make segregation at the stadium a legal fact, but he was waiting to see how things developed. The major league club was still hoping the pickets would just go away, and Will was left in the middle, trying to run a ball club.

It was hard to know what was happening in regard to the murder case. The SBI and the IRS had backed out of the case and turned it over to the local police. They said they were convinced it was in no way connected with the statewide bootlegging operation, and they had turned all the results of their investigations over to the Centerville police. That meant Boris and Will were still suspects. At least, the local detectives had been out a couple of times to talk to Will and Boris, and once more they'd been talking to me. It really was getting tiring, and I still wished they could forget the whole thing.

The team was still in first place, but for the last couple of weeks Donald had taken over for Millard as bat boy. Now, I never thought I'd miss Millard, but it did seem strange not to have him on the field running to get the bats. And Donald, he was about the worst bat boy possible. You'd think someone as smart as Donald could go pick up bats, but he was usually running his mouth to one of the players and he'd forget to pick them up. Then Fitzie would have to cuss him out for not doing his job. Anyway, Millard would be back in a few days, and then Donald could go back to selling Cokes.

Millard had been sent to Raleigh for some tests, and it was the night we had all the trouble that I went and sat with the councilman in his box seats and asked him where Millard was. The councilman patted me on the shoulder like he usually did and told me about the tests in Raleigh.

"Tom, Mrs. Waller just hasn't been well for the last year or so, and she can't look after Millard like she used to. I just don't have the time to take away from the drugstore. We've been talking to a few schools about sending him where he can get the proper supervision. You remember last winter when he pulled down the fence and hurt himself. Well, Mrs. Waller was sick that day, and Millard shouldn't have been out of the house. And that wasn't the first time he's wandered out without anyone knowing it. We're afraid he'll hurt himself seriously if he isn't given the proper direction."

It was something of a shock to hear the councilman say this. I'd be the first to admit that Millard wasn't quite right, but I couldn't see them sending him away. "Wouldn't you miss him?"

"Of course, Tom, of course. But sometimes you have to do what's necessary. Maybe he'd be better off in a school."

"Gee, it wouldn't seem right without Millard here at the park."

"I know. This ball park gives Millard more pleasure than you could ever imagine. But fortunately, we don't have to make a decision yet. Millard will be home at the end of the week, and we'll decide something in the fall."

"I guess it's hard to think about, but it just seems Millard would be better off with his mother and father." The councilman looked at me, and I guess he thought it was strange, because I was living with my uncle. The one thing I didn't want the previous summer was to go live with my own father. I guess that's why I felt so strongly about Millard leaving. He liked the ball park almost as much as I did, and I couldn't see anyone having to leave it.

In the fourth inning I wandered out to look at the pickets. Nothing was happening, and I stopped by Maggie's ticket booth to check her change. She was still working at the park selling tickets, but things between her and Will had not picked up. They spoke to each other and everything, but most nights when the team was on the road, Will would sit home with me and watch television. She was talking about leaving town, and she'd started sending applications to different law schools.

I probably should have been more observant and said something to Will about getting more policemen for the night, but I figured those two guys hanging around the park for a couple of days couldn't do any real harm. I was wrong. As it was we had only old Mr. Horace as the policeman on duty, and he doesn't even wear a gun. We'd had our share of curiosity seekers, people just coming out to stare at the pickets, but the two men in the parking lot were different. They were rough looking, and they stood beside their car and seemed to be counting the number of pickets each night. I had never seen either of them before, but I let it pass and didn't say anything to Will.

The trouble started about the fifth inning. I was out at Mag-

131

gie's booth talking to her when I saw about five or six cars drive up. They were squealing tires as they came around the corner, and you just knew that nobody was coming to a ball game in that much of a hurry. All the pickets stopped and stared as the cars drove up in front of the stadium. The cars were full of men, and they piled out. I counted twenty-five. The two men who had been hanging around the parking lot seemed to be in charge. I could see there was going to be some trouble, and I rushed back to the office to get Will.

When I came back with Will the whites were leaning on the cars, chewing on toothpicks and yelling a few things at the protesters. The marchers said nothing back, and they continued their marching. You could tell they were a little nervous, but they tried to ignore the comments. Mr. Johnson had gone back to the front gate when the cars had driven up, wondering if the whites were going to come in, but seeing the situation, he picked up his sign and started marching again.

Mr. Horace, the policeman, had followed Will out, but he wasn't going to be much good for anything he was so old. Will yelled out to the whites, and he knew one of the men who was in charge.

"Travis, why don't you and your friends go home. We don't want any trouble here."

The other man sneered back. "Listen, baseball man. We've got as much right here as them burr heads. If you ain't gonna do anything about 'em, we just might."

Will repeated his request that they leave, but they didn't. "Baseball man, if these here niggers can march, so can we. It's a free country, and we aim to protest along with 'em."

And then the whites on a signal started coming for the marchers. They walked slowly, and there were two of the toughs for every one of the Negroes. They fell in alongside of the picketers, elbowing them and making comments.

I'd started reading up on some of this stuff and talking to the marchers about what would happen if somebody tried to get violent with them, and they all talked about Gandhi and Martin

132

Luther King and the principle of passive resistance. It looked like it might get a test.

Will was getting worried, and he walked over to Maggie's ticket booth and told her to close up. He was speaking softly, but the voice didn't sound like Will's. As she came out of the booth he spoke again. "Call the police and hurry. This thing's going to blow real soon." Mr. Horace was still standing alongside Will, but he hadn't said anything. One policeman wasn't going to be able to handle the situation.

We heard some commotion around the side of the stadium, and it was almost as if the whites had been waiting for it. The leader, Travis, stopped and looked over in the direction of the noise. He yelled over to Mr. Horace, "Officer, there seems to be a fight around the corner. I think you ought to check it out."

I went out into the parking lot where I could see what was happening. Two white boys were fighting, although it was more like they were just rolling in the grass and wrestling. Mr. Horace looked relieved that he could leave the front of the stadium, and he shuffled down to the end of the grandstand. It had to be a put-up job to get the policeman out of the area.

Will was trying to get me to leave, but there was no way I was going. At first there was just some shoving and pushing as the whites marched alongside the Negroes. None of the toughs seemed to have any weapons, and I thought all they wanted was to break up the signs and scare the demonstrators. But apparently Reverend Tillman got them riled, his being white, and one of the white guys started shoving him in the face and spitting on him. Will was getting edgy, for the situation wasn't good, and when Maggie came back and told him the police were on the way, he looked a little more relieved. He told Maggie to go back to the stands, but she stayed right there. I think she wanted to do something, but there was really the question of what anybody could do. A few fans were looking from the concession area, but most of them were staying back.

Reverend Tillman had tripped or been pushed, and he had fallen to his knees by this time. When one of the whites kicked him, it was more than Mr. Johnson could take. He went up and pushed the white man away and was helping Reverend Tillman to his feet when all hell broke loose. The whites started punching the colored people and hitting them with the signs, and none of the Negroes was fighting back. Most were just trying to protect themselves from the punches, but some had fallen to the ground. Mr. Johnson was lying on the ground, and there were all these white men and nobody else to help.

Then somebody started kicking Mr. Johnson. Two guys were standing over him, and one was kicking him while the other just kept spitting down on top of him. Up to this time, Will had been holding people back, because there wasn't much he could do, and the police were supposed to be coming. But then something must have snapped. I know I've never seen him that angry, but he rushed the two men over Mr. Johnson and pushed them away from his gatekeeper. Then Maggie rushed out and started trying to get some of the whites off the Reverend Tillman, but it was doing no good. It seemed as if half the whites jumped on Will and were really beating him, and I saw one man punch Maggie in the stomach and throw her to the ground. I guess that's when I caused the forfeit.

I rushed back in the park. I'd never been on the field during a game in my life, and the Owls were at bat, but I had to do something. I really thought they were going to kill Will, and I didn't know where the police were. Mr. Johnson was hurt, Maggie was being hurt, and I couldn't fight.

I was running, running as fast as I could. Yet, it seemed as if I were in a movie where they slow the action and all you see are certain frames of the picture and it takes too long to reach the next frame. I was trying to run, and as I came back into the stadium and down the concourse to the field, I passed by the concession stand. But it was as if I never passed the stand, and all I could see was the "Coca-Cola 10¢" sign, staring me in the face, staring at me for hours. And I kept trying to pass the Coca-Cola sign. The next thing I remember is Miss Elmira. Only she wasn't standing still. She was moving fast, too fast, and she had her broom and was going in the opposite direction, and I couldn't understand what Miss Elmira was doing running while I seemed to be standing still.

Everybody was staring at me as I reached the field and jumped over the fence separating the stands from the playing field. I had to get to Fitzie, but it had been hours since I left Will outside, and I had almost forgotten what was happening. There was Fitzie in the third base coach's box. The ball game stopped as I tried to move fast enough to get to Fitzie. As I ran, I was yelling and screaming, "They're hurting Will. They're hurting Will and Maggie." Thinking back I don't know how Fitz understood what I was saying. I guess he knew something was up, because many of the fans were at the top of the grandstand, looking over the edge at the people fighting. But he didn't say a thing, and I saw him wave to the team on the bench, and Boris and all the players rushed off the field with Fitzie. I'm not sure a lot of people in the stands knew what was happening, except the entire Centerville Owls team was following some fourteen-year-old kid to the parking lot.

We got there just in time, because nobody had come to help except Miss Elmira who was standing over Maggie with her broom. Two white toughs were standing back, not knowing what to do with this fierce colored woman daring them to come forward. I could see Will on the ground with blood flowing from his mouth. Two men were on top of him, pounding him with their fists. And I knew I had to help Will. I started for him when I felt someone roughly push me away. I thought one of the white guys had jumped me, but I looked around and it was Boris. I couldn't understand why he was pushing me away when I saw him staring at my hand. I looked down, and for some reason I was carrying a bat. I must have picked it up when I was on the field yelling for Fitzie to come and carried it back. I suppose I was going to use it. Boris only looked at me for an instant, and then he was on top of the men who were on Will.

With eighteen Centerville Owls taking on twenty-five white guys, it turned into an even fight. People from the stands were

135

coming out and cheering the team. The Owls were winning when I heard the sirens. The group of white toughs heard the sirens also, and they pulled back and started for their cars. The Owls wanted to follow, but Fitz yelled for the team to stop. He said later he was worried one of his players might get hurt, and he didn't know how he was going to explain to the front office that the team had been in a fight in the parking lot. The whites' cars were driving off as the police turned the corner, but the leader, Travis, yelled out as the car drove by. "You nigger loving team, nobody's ever going to come out here again, and I aim to make sure." He was off before the police could follow.

That was the ball game. The Durham manager offered to let the Owls keep playing, but the umpires said they couldn't. It was a league rule. I don't really think the Owls were in much of a mood to keep playing anyway, and I couldn't have cared less about the game.

Boris and I were leaning over Will, and he was talking but not making much sense. He got to his feet when the ambulance came, and I guess he was better. Maggie wasn't hurt too bad, and she was wiping some of the blood from his face. I really wanted to go to the hospital with him, but Will kept saying I had to stay. He wanted me to close up the ball park, so I didn't go. Besides, Maggie was going with him, and she could make sure everything was OK.

I wasn't sure how I was going to be able to close the park. My hands were shaking so much I could hardly open the door to the office, and I just sat at the desk shaking. That's why I'm glad Fitzie and Boris came in and sat with me. For a while with all the ambulances and police cars around, there were more people around Centerville Stadium than had been there in a month. Except nobody was interested in baseball. The police did keep some cars around. Fitzie and Boris hadn't even bothered to get dressed but kept sitting with me in the office. That was good because the phone kept ringing from news people and others that had just heard there had been a riot. Boris answered the phone and tried to explain everything.

Fitzie was sitting, talking to me, telling me stories about some of the things that had happened to him in baseball. I'd always thought Fitzie was sort of mean and gruff, but he was really funny that night. I knew he was trying to get my mind off Will. I tried to apologize to him for running out on the field and causing the forfeit, but he said he was glad I did it. Every once in a while Boris would call the hospital, but there was still no word on Will and the others who had been hurt.

After a while Fitzie had to make some calls, and he phoned Mr. Carmody long distance. I could tell from the conversation that Mr. Carmody wasn't pleased. And then Fitz called the league president in Wilson to tell him about the forfeit and explain why the umpires had made their decision. Finally, we received word from the hospital that Will was all right and Maggie was taking him home. I didn't ride my bike home that night. While Fitzie and Boris were getting dressed, I locked all the gates and then put my bike in the office as Boris drove me home. Will didn't look so good, but he was smiling so I knew he was all right. Maggie told me to make sure he didn't stay up, and so when she left he went right to bed. I had some trouble getting to sleep myself, but finally I drifted off.

The next morning the paper really played it up big. The headlines read, "Riot at Centerville Stadium," and they had a picture of the Owls fighting right on the front page. I suppose the story was accurate, but I think they played it up a little worse than it was. Newspapers tend to do things like that. The story said nobody had suffered serious injuries although two people had been admitted to the hospital, Mr. Johnson with cracked ribs and Reverend Tillman who complained of dizziness. The police had apprehended some of the white guys, but they had been released on bail.

It's a good thing we didn't have a game that day, for Will was late coming down for breakfast, and I could tell he didn't feel so good. His eyes were puffy, and he moved like an old man. He mumbled at me and went and fixed himself a cup of coffee. I asked if he wanted any Rice Krispies, but he just shook his head. When he saw the headlines, he groaned. I could see it was worrying him. He didn't say too much until his second cup of coffee, but then he talked about how the story would scare off a lot of people.

He took the paper and stared at it for a while, and I knew he was thinking something. Finally, I asked him. "What you gonna do?"

"I think I'm going to integrate the stands."

This shocked me. Up until now he was just waiting for things to cool down. Now, he was changing 100 percent. I couldn't believe it. "You can't do that."

"Why not? What's it going to hurt now? With this story and the threat of violence, we're going to lose a lot of fans anyway. I'm just sick of having the ball park a scene of picketing and fighting. The team's integrated, we've been sitting the colored wives in the box seats, and our concession stand is integrated. The demonstrations aren't going to stop. Let's just go ahead and solve the problem and let people sit where they want."

"What do you think will happen?"

"Well, we won't need to worry about the two groups who were there last night. Those whites aren't going to buy a ticket to come in and protest. They'll make a few phone calls to us, but that will be about it. The Negroes who are picketing will come to about one game, but that will be it. They're just trying to make an issue. Most of our old colored fans will come back, and they'll sit where they always sat. We'll lose some whites, but I think we've already lost those who really care about segregation. And this year will be bad, but there's always next season, and maybe by then people will have forgotten. But if we keep holding out, the pickets will stay and nobody will ever forget."

"Do you think Mr. Carmody will go along?"

"I don't see why not. He's let me handle this all along. Somebody's got to make a decision, and it might as well be me. I know the big club must be sick of all this trouble."

Late in the morning Will talked to Councilman Waller about his decision to integrate the stands. The councilman was dead set

138

against integration. "Will, I understand how you feel. I know you don't want any more trouble out at the park, but I think I can assure you the city will put enough policeman around so that last night's incident won't be repeated. I just can't believe that integrating your stands will cause you anything but more trouble. Your fans may love baseball, but they are Southerners first, and I believe most of them will desert you if you go ahead with what you are planning."

But Councilman Waller couldn't talk Will out of his decision, and I was surprised that he said he would back Will up. He would pull back his resolution for the City Council that would have enforced segregation at the ball park. Will told the councilman that he would have to get Mr. Carmody's approval, and a final decision should be reached shortly.

It was early afternoon when Will called Mr. Carmody. He had been preparing for some time what he planned to say, but when he phoned it was apparent that Mr. Carmody was waiting for his call. I didn't listen in, although I would have liked to, but Will told me just about everything the farm director told him. Will explained his position to Mr. Carmody and why he wanted to integrate, but the farm director would not give in to Will's wishes.

"Will, I certainly can see your side, but right now I'm afraid the decision is out of both your and my hands. We've had a good deal of calls from national news people wanting to know what we're going to do, and Mr. Fleer is terribly concerned over the situation. He supports everything you've done so far, Will, and he's been impressed with how you've handled a very trying situation. But when I talked with him this morning, he felt a decision on the Centerville problem should be his. Basically, he doesn't want to appear he's giving in to pressure. He's having a meeting with me and a few of the major stockholders later in the day, and we're going to try to reach some sort of decision. I'll certainly relay your feelings, but so much is involved now. I'll call back later in the day, and we should have reached some conclusion."

Will and I sat in the office most of the afternoon, and late in the

139

day Maggie came by as did Councilman Waller. Both were surprised that the major league club had not readily gone along with Will. It was 5:30 before the phone rang again, and it was Mr. Carmody. The farm director did most of the talking.

"Will, I'm afraid desegregating your stands is out. Opinion was pretty unanimous against it. You know, Mr. Fleer was very unhappy last year when he was forced to trade for colored ball players he felt weren't up to the caliber of his other players. He felt that his farm system would have developed one or two in the next couple of years who would have been ready for the big leagues. He just doesn't want it to seem that every time there are pickets or protest he gives in. He wants to make it clear that he's running a baseball team, not a civil rights springboard.

"We want you to arrange a meeting with the head of the local NAACP and try to get them to remove the pickets so that we can talk over the winter. Make it clear that only through negotiation will we discuss integration. Will, you realize that we have four other farm clubs in the south, and all of them have segregated seating. If we give in here, every other club owned by Mr. Fleer will have pickets springing up tomorrow night. We're here to give the fans baseball, not end segregation in public stadiums. Other major league clubs have farm teams in the South, and they're worried about your situation. They've been calling us. We could do a job at destroying many minor league clubs at a time when many are terribly weak already. I know you've had to go through a great deal down there, but we can only ask you to bear up the rest of the season. We'll have an official release ready tomorrow for you to give to the press."

After Will hung up, he relayed the conversation to us. I looked at Maggie and could tell she wasn't happy, but Mr. Carmody was right. There was no way we could integrate. Will and Councilman Waller talked about the decision, and they arranged for extra police protection. The next day Mr. Waller arranged a meeting with the local NAACP, but they would not agree to stop picketing. I could have told them that. That afternoon the offi-

cial release came from the major league club, and Will handed it
out to the press. It read:

*The Centerville Owls will continue their policy of separate
seating for the races in Centerville Stadium. While the club
recognizes the desires of the Negro citizen, it feels as a member
of the entire community, it cannot change traditions that have
lasted close to a hundred years. Moreover, it feels it is slightly
presumptuous for the club to try to impose on these traditions.
This does not mean that the Centerville team is turning its back
on the Negro fan, and it can assure members of the Negro
community it will be happy to negotiate when the atmosphere of
intimidation has passed. Over the winter the club will review its
policy, and hopefully some decision acceptable to the total
community can be reached. But it must be repeated that this
decision can only be reached if the demonstrations and protests
are stopped. We hope that the community will forget the inci-
dents of the past weeks and make baseball, not race, its concern,
and root for the Owls as they try to bring a pennant and credit to
the best city in the Carolina League, Centerville.*

11

It still sits there, the huge concrete arches, the tarnished bronze name plate, the stark naked light towers. But it is dead now, whatever was there has long since departed, and it is now only a shell, only a memory. You are surprised that they left it standing, for old things, things that have memories, are meant to be torn down, meant to make way for progress. You debate whether to get out, but you do, and you walk past the empty sarcophagi which were once disguised as ticket booths. You walk past the gates that no longer have locks for there is nothing to lock in or out.

It was once alive with people, with men running and crowds cheering. And there was laughter, and shouts, and boos, and occasionally tears. But it was life, each year renewed to try again, to once more struggle, hope, pray, and finally accept. But some-

thing changed, and there are no more men, no more people watching their battles. All that remains is a structure with seats rotting and a field overgrown with weeds. High on the roof a box that chronicled the history of life on the grass is empty, for no one needs to report the history of the dead.

And you would like to yell, or cheer, or whistle, or do anything to provide a contrast to the silence. But you sit and wait, wait for an old man who may tell you what happened here many years before when everything was still alive.

"HEY,Tom, what's happening with the murder case?"
"Not much. They haven't been around to talk to me or Will in a long time."

"I heard they want to talk to Millard."

"Millard? You've got to be kidding."

"Naw, my father knows somebody on the detective force, and they got a phone call from someone who remembered seeing Millard wandering around the ball park one night about the same time as he turned up missing."

"Well, that's stupid. Millard couldn't hurt anybody."

"They still want to talk to him."

"Gee, they won't be able to understand him if they do talk to him. And I'll bet the councilman won't like that." I didn't like it either. Why were they pulling Millard into that thing? Nobody in the world cared that my father was dead.

I looked over at Monty. "Do you think they'll ever drop the case?"

"My father says they'd like to, but they're still getting pressure from the federal and state people to do something. Councilman Waller has been pushing them to close it, but they won't."

Monty and I were riding in the back of the trunk as we talked. Monty and I always talked in the trunk. He changed the subject and asked me how Will was holding up. Things hadn't been going well at the park.

"He's still smiling. But I don't think he feels that way inside."

Monty spit out of the back of the trunk and tried to hit a car following us. He missed but kept talking. "You think we'll lose the team?"

"Naw. Mr. Carmody already told Will they'd keep the team here no matter what." But it was sure that nobody was coming to the games.

145

We were riding to one of our playground league games, and that's why we were in the back of the trunk. It's not Little League or Pony League or any of those teams that have uniforms and play in neat little parks. It's just recreation department baseball, and we play in the different school yards. It's for guys thirteen to fifteen who aren't good enough for some of the other teams. But we like it.

Monty and I always ride in the trunk. If we didn't there'd be ten people in the front and that's a little crowded. The good thing about riding in the trunk is we can drag bats on the concrete and make faces at the people in the cars behind. It's just generally fun. Sitting on bats and balls can be uncomfortable, but we usually stuff them up behind the spare tire. Monty likes to mouth cuss words at the people in the cars behind. I'm not sure if that counts as cussing, since he doesn't actually say the word, but the people behind think he's cussing and he gets a kick out of it. The one problem with the trunk is railroad tracks. Peaches, who is driving the car, doesn't slow down for railroad tracks, and the trunk hood can bounce around and hit our heads. What we have to do is while one of us drags a bat on the pavement, the other will hold his bat straight up so the trunk lid will hit that. We used to drag our sneakers, but it was wearing down the rubber so we switched to bats.

Monty and I sometimes talk about whether we might die of carbon monoxide poisoning, but with it being only three or four miles to one of our games, I don't think that could happen. Monty says his mother doesn't like him riding in the trunk. She's afraid he might bounce out, but it sure beats riding in the front. To begin with it's a '47 Pontiac, not one of your more stylish cars, but the main reason is all the people. Also, I don't think J. R. Flynn, our first baseman, uses deodorant.

Peaches, who drives the car, is our manager, and he's also the playground director. He likes going to the games because it gets him off the playground where the only thing you can do all day is play Chinese checkers or make a potholder. That gets old after a while. Peaches is a college student at Elon, and about the only

146

exciting thing he does back at the playground is to roll the hairs on his legs into little balls and then light them with matches. He hasn't burnt himself yet.

Our team isn't very good. In fact, I guess you could say it's bad, but then we don't have enough people. That's why I play center field. We've only got about seven guys who really want to play ball, and every game we'll have to round up some eleven- or twelve-year-old who's playing tether ball or making a pot holder and ask him if he'd like to play for us. If he says no, then Peaches will go up and tell him if he doesn't play he'll be thrown off the playground. That may not be quite right, but like I said, Peaches likes to get off the playground, and you need nine people on a team. Well, with these kids who don't want to play we'll put them in right field or left field, and since what I do best is run, I'm in center field to chase after balls when they miss them. They miss a lot, and I run a lot, and we don't win many games. But we haven't forfeited one yet, thanks to Peaches.

Monty plays third base. He's pretty good and should be playing shortstop, only Rabbit Johnson is shortstop. Rabbit's no good, but he won't play unless he can be shortstop. He also brings along his brother who's sixteen and too old, but he's our pitcher and can hit, and I don't think they check birth certificates in this league anyway. I've seen guys playing for the team over in the mill village who are nineteen. They haven't lost a game yet. We can't protest because we've got Rabbit's brother, and most of the teams in our league have illegal players anyway. Donald is our catcher, which is just great with everyone. He's not that good, but he likes to think he's tough and gritty. We're more than willing to let anybody catch if they want to prove they're tough and gritty.

Monty started talking about the ball park. "Things aren't so much fun around there lately, are they?"

"Yeah." Have you got any idea how bad a ball park is when there aren't any people in it? And I don't mean after a game, because it's nice to wander around when everyone has left. I mean when a ball game is going on and nobody's in the stands.

147

Or, at least, only a very few fans. It's got to be the most depressing thing I've ever seen, and ever since the riot, only a few were coming out. Will tried to act jolly, but I know if he could have he would have just liked to break down and cry. There were now about two hundred people who came to the games, and they were all spread around. They made so little noise it was like going to a funeral

There just wasn't anything Will could do either. Most people were scared to come out, and some people in town had been spreading rumors that the white toughs who started the fight were going to get anybody coming to the games. Some fans had even gotten phone calls. I don't know what would have happened if Will's plan to integrate had gone through. The colored pickets were still outside, and it had just turned into an awful situation.

About the only thing happening was the Owls were back in first place. But in a way this made it even worse, for with finally a pennant contender for Centerville, nobody was coming out. The team was playing as good as any Owl team had ever played, but even they were feeling a little low, because it's no fun to play in front of empty stands.

It wasn't much fun to work in the office either. That was because of the phone calls. We were getting them there and at home, and I didn't know what to do. Will said hang up, which I did, but after a while it got kind of scary. Someone would call and not say anything or breathe heavily. If they did say something it wasn't nice, and I never knew if they really meant it. Of course, we could have let the phone just ring, but it might have been somebody wanting to come to the game, and how can you not answer a ringing telephone?

Other things had happened. Somebody wrote "nigger lover" in front of the park with paint that didn't come off, and after a game one night, we went home and found three of our windows had been broken with rocks.

Monty was dragging a tire iron on the street, seeing if he could

148

make sparks, when we went over a railroad track which almost made him drop it. He stopped and placed it back under the spare tire. We were almost at the playground on the south side of town. "How's your grandmother doing?" he asked.

"Much better. She's out of the hospital and back home with my mother."

Ten days earlier, while the team was on the road, Will had driven east to visit my grandmother. She had been put in the hospital, but now she was out of danger. I was glad, because I didn't like funerals. While Will was gone, I had spent two nights with Monty. I could have stayed home. I usually don't mind staying by myself, but with all the phone calls and everything, I felt better going over and staying with him. It was fun too. Monty's parents went out one night, and we sneaked a couple of his father's cans of beer and drank them. I don't know if I was drunk, but my head sure was spinning.

We got to the playground OK. Neither Monty nor I died of carbon monoxide poisoning, but we lost the game, 16 to 3. It's mainly because Donald had something like eight passed balls, and everybody would strike out but then run to first base. Midway through the game Rabbit got mad at Donald for all the errors, and Donald called Rabbit a "pansy." Rabbit quit the team right there, and we played the last three innings with only eight men. After the same, with Rabbit still mad at Donald, they had Rabbit sit in the trunk with me. I don't really like Rabbit that much, so there wasn't much to talk about.

On the way back, Peaches dropped Monty, Donald, and me at the ball park. It was too early for me to start on my tickets, and I walked out to the field to watch batting practice. I saw Boris shagging fly balls in the outfield, and I decided to go out and talk with him. I'd been talking a lot with Boris lately. With Will having so much on his mind, I didn't want to bother him with my problems, and Boris seemed to understand. Also, I felt I should tell him what I'd heard from Monty.

"Boris."

"Hi, Tommy. How'd the team do?"

149

"Oh, we lost."

"Too bad."

"Yeah. Hey, did you hear that the police want to talk to Millard?"

"No. Why?"

"Seems they heard he was messing around here the day my father turned up missing."

"Did you see him that last night you saw your father?"

"Not that I recall. You know, if my father had never come to town, I don't guess we'd have all these problems."

"You can't always get what you want, Tommy. And besides, the pickets would still be here."

"Yeah, I guess so. But why can't things stay the way you want them to be? It was better before."

"The pickets don't think so."

"Oh, I know all that. Maggie's talked to me about segregation. I guess it isn't fair that colored people can't sit where they want to, but why do they have to start with the Centerville Owls. It isn't fair to Will."

"You're probably right, Tommy, but where do you start? Things aren't fair to a lot of people."

"Are things fair to you, Boris?"

"Tommy, I'm doing all I ever wanted, chasing after a white ball and trying to hit it when someone throws it to me."

And with that a fly ball came toward the outfield, and Boris went after it. I went back toward the stands, because I wasn't really supposed to be on the field during batting practice. Donald was sitting in the box seats watching practice, and I went and sat beside him. "You gonna be selling Cokes, tonight?"

"Naw," he answered. "Someone might spill them for me. I'll probably sit with Monty on the scoreboard."

It looked like Donald was still mad at me, and I didn't know why. I'd paid him back for the Cokes. Besides, the reason he wasn't selling drinks was nobody was much in the stands to buy them. It had nothing to do with my spilling his tray.

150

It all involved Millard. It had happened three nights earlier when some of the toughs who'd been involved in the fight actually bought tickets to the game. I think they were a little drunk, and they didn't come to watch the game. They were in the park just to cause trouble. Most of the game they were riding the team, yelling for the Owls to strike out. But that's part of baseball, and if somebody wants to yell something at the team and he's bought a ticket, he can do it. Even some of our regular fans do that.

But midway through the game they started making fun of Millard. They were mocking the funny way he runs back with the bats and just generally not being very nice to him. I could see Millard didn't like it. Some of the players were yelling up to the two guys, telling them to shut up, but that just caused them to yell more.

I was sitting in the stands wondering what I could do to help Millard when Donald came up and sat with me. He'd been trying to sell Cokes, but the fans weren't buying very many, and the ones he had were getting hot. I asked Donald if I couldn't sell some for him, and he said sure. I walked over to where the two guys were sitting and yelling at Millard, and I pretended to trip. I spilled Donald's Cokes all over them. You could tell they thought I had done it on purpose, but I apologized like I hadn't meant it. Mr. Horace, the policeman, was nearby, the first time I'd ever seen him where someone might need him, so the two guys couldn't do anything. But their clothes were all wet, and they left in a few minutes.

I wandered to the office and started setting up my tickets. It didn't take much time with only Maggie selling. She and Will were getting along a little better, but it didn't look as if things would ever get back like they were. I'd heard that Maggie was now dating a lawyer in town, but I didn't tell Will. He may have known anyway. Mr. Johnson was back on the front gate. He'd spent only a few days in the hospital after the riot. He occasionally would pick up a sign and march in front, but even the enthusiasm of the protesters had fallen way off. With nobody coming to the games, there wasn't much to protest about.

As I worked on my tickets, I kept thinking about Millard. What could he tell the police? I tried to think back to the final night I had seen my father. Somehow Millard was associated, but I couldn't put my finger on it. Then I remembered. It had been at the clubhouse. My father had wanted some cigarettes. We were in the outfield, and by then he had trouble standing up. He was still talking about taking me with him when he demanded I get him the cigarettes. I made the long walk to the stands.

That's where I'd seen Millard. I had first gone to the concession stand for cigarettes, but they were out. However, I knew there were some in the clubhouse. I stopped by the office for the keys, and as I headed for the clubhouse I heard a noise. I looked up, and there was Millard. I called out to him, but he ran away. Yes, Millard had been there that night. Then I had gone to the clubhouse and picked up a pack of cigarettes. But I did not remember locking it. Did I leave the clubhouse open? Had someone been in after me and taken a piece of pipe?

I tried to push the thoughts from my mind. Soon the season would be over, and everybody would forget the murder and the demonstrations. Then we could think about a new season with none of these problems. Maggie came in and picked up her tickets, and I went out to the stands to watch the game.

12

The old man walks in very slowly, and you are surprised at how he has aged. But then he must be eighty now. He comes closer, and the eyes are alert, still clear, and he calls your name and he shakes your hand. He is not surprised that you have come back. After all these years he said he expected you. Then before you can say what you want to know, he begins a story. You listen.

He tells about a boy who lived with his uncle and loved a town and a ball park. When he was thirteen it was all threatened by a man who was his father. The boy thought the man was going to take him away from everything he loved. Then there was a murder, and the father was dead. The boy stayed. Only two people in town knew who had committed the murder.

One was a mentally retarded man who had slipped out on the night of the murder and had gone to the ball park. He saw the murder, and he knew of a grave, but because he was retarded, he had difficulty making people understand. He kept going back to the grave, and one January when he was climbing around a fence, it tumbled over and the body came up. Only then was he able to make his father, a councilman, understand what he had seen.

The other who knew of the murder was an outfielder, a burly, hairy man who could hit homeruns and was a career minor leaguer. But he would say nothing until the September of the following year when everything started falling in place for the police.

S O many things happened that night, but what comes through over everything else is lying in the parking lot on top of Millard while he's crying and I'm trying to hold him down. I was telling him everything was going to be OK, even though I knew it wasn't. Finally, Will and Maggie came out and found us and took us back inside the park.

It was the last game of the season, and last games are both sad and happy. They're sad because it's the last time you'll see some of the people for six or seven months, and some of them you'll never see again. Over the winter they release a lot of the players who didn't do too good, and some of the fans move away or die or don't come back. So usually on the last night Will puts on "Auld Lang Syne" over the PA system, and everybody hangs around the park a little longer than usual saying goodbye to people they might not see again. The last games are happy because it means you've gotten through another season, which is always a good feeling. If you've done poorly, there's always next year.

It seemed like it was going to be like the end of any other season, except with all the racial problems we didn't have as many fans to say goodbye to. I know Will was looking forward to another year when he could do away with all the racial stuff and not have to worry about a murder.

We had no idea what was going to happen, although I guess it should have been some clue when Mr. Carmody called and said he'd be in for the final game. There was nothing wrong with Mr. Carmody coming in, but a farm director never comes in for the last game of the season. The players have played 140 games, so everybody knows what they can do, and all the team cares about is finishing the game so they can start the long drives home. We didn't really think much about his visit, although I did ask Will at breakfast.

"Will, why do you think Mr. Carmody's coming in today?"

"Don't really know."

"What'd he say?"

"Wants to talk to me, the councilman, and Fitzie."

"Aren't you worried it might be something bad?"

"No. The year hasn't been all bad, considering the problems. Now hurry up and finish your breakfast. You're going to be late."

Will was rushing me through breakfast because school was back in session. I don't know if I was ever ready for school to start back, but I wished it hadn't started Tuesday. I had to go to school, be there until 3:30, rush out to the ball park, help shine the shoes, and get tickets ready as best I could. And then I wouldn't get home until 11 or 11:30.

Eighth grade had been bad, but I couldn't believe the amount of work the ninth-grade teachers were assigning. Of course, some of them were doing it to impress you on how hard the ninth grade was going to be, but I don't think the Latin or algebra teachers were trying to impress anybody. Here I was only four days into school, and I was already behind. I had Monty and Donald in a couple of my classes, but nobody was goofing off the first week. Who wants to be on the bad side of a teacher right away? Donald acted like he was trying for the American Legion citizenship award the way he was brown nosing teachers. Monty and I knew it wasn't for real, but you'd have thought the teachers would have been able to see through some of his stuff. I just tried to find a seat in the back of the room where the teachers wouldn't see me and would have a hard time remembering my name.

Now that we were ninth graders we had to act differently. Well, we were the senior class in junior high school, and the principal kept talking about how we had to set an example for the classes under us and how we had to show school spirit. Can you believe it, but some of the people in our class actually went along with all that? Even if you tried to goof off or do anything, somebody would go "shhhh" at you and give a dirty look. I just knew the ninth grade wasn't going to be much fun.

At lunch that Friday, Donald said he was coming out to the game, it being the last one. He hadn't been working the last couple of weeks, so he'd stopped coming to the games. It didn't make much sense selling Cokes if no one was around to buy them. But I was sorry he wasn't coming to the games. We needed as many people as we could get in the stands, whether they paid or not.

After lunch Monty and I went and threw rocks at a tree. It was too hot to throw a football around, and we sure didn't feel like sitting in the cafeteria where it smelled so bad. Donald went off and talked to some girl. There wasn't much doubt that Donald was going to be a pill the entire year. He'd even bought a pair of Weejun loafers which only the rich kids wore. I sure didn't know who he was trying to impress, but Monty and I talked about it while we threw rocks. We were going to have to do something to bring him back to normal. We were thinking of throwing spit-balls at him during English class.

While we were throwing rocks, Monty brought up the investigation. The only thing I'd heard the last month or so was that Millard and the councilman had been down to the police station a couple of times. Monty hit dead center with a rock as he spoke.

"My father says the police are about to make a move."

"Naw."

"Yeah. With this being the team's last day in town they got to do something. He says they're going to ask Boris to stay around a few more days."

"I don't believe it."

"Well, just wait and see."

"Aw, you're full of it, Monty." With that the bell rang, and we both went to class.

After school I rode my bike over to the park and went immediately to the clubhouse. During the last two periods I'd been thinking about Mr. Carmody's visit and what Monty had said about Boris, and really I was a little worried. I started shining the shoes, and that was one good thing. It was the last time I'd have to do that for seven months. The players were arriving, and I was darkening the shoes with polish when Boris came in. I wandered over to his locker.

"Boris, you worried about Mr. Carmody coming in?"

He gave a big laugh. "Why should I be?"

"He might release you."

"Well, if he does, there's not much I can do about it. I don't think worrying will do much good. Besides, I've had a pretty good year."

I changed the subject. "Boris, I heard the police might ask you to stay in town."

He looked up at me as he pulled up his socks. "Tommy, we'll just have to wait and see what happens on that, now won't we?"

I was about to say something else to Boris when I heard Fitzie come in. I didn't see him, but you didn't need to see him to know it was Fitz. You could tell by the sound of his tobacco juice. There's nobody else that can spit tobacco juice with as much squish. Fitzie yelled out at me.

"Goddammit. Look at these shoes. Two damn years and you still don't know how to polish spikes. Tom, I think you're absolutely hopeless." I stopped talking to Boris and decided I'd better do the shoes the best I could for the final game.

You'd have thought by the last game of the season Fitzie might be in a good mood. But no. He still acted the same. And the team had won the pennant too. It still didn't change him. Everybody said Fitzie had done a good job. Winning a pennant usually means you've done a good job, but the scouts who came to town said we didn't really have the best team in the league. I'm not sure how scouts know these things, but most of them said the Hi-Toms had the best team. They said Fitzie had gotten more out of his players than anybody else could have. I think Fitzie knew he had done a good job, because the final month his ulcer hadn't been acting up as much.

Most of the players were cleaning out their lockers and putting

158

their extra equipment in their cars. Most would be leaving for home immediately after the game. Boris's old car was already packed. He said he was planning to drive north all night long. That was unless the Centerville police asked him to stay. I finished up quickly in the clubhouse, because I wanted to be around the office when Mr. Carmody came in.

It was 6:30 before a cab with Mr. Carmody drove up. Will was waiting for him and shook his hand.

"Good to see you."

"Will, good to see you. Flight was delayed about an hour, so I won't have too much time. I've got a flight leaving immediately after the game."

The two walked up to the field and looked at the players warming up, but Mr. Carmody wanted to get to business. "Will, I'd like to use your office. First, I'll talk with Fitz. When I've finished, I'd like you and Councilman Waller to come in for a little chat."

"No problem at all, Mr. Carmody. I'll have Tom get Fitz." Will nodded to me and I ran toward the field.

Fitzie was on the field hitting infield, and I was about to yell out to him, when I stopped short. Down by the dugout three men were talking. I saw Boris, Councilman Waller, and the local chief of police. The chief had not been to a game all season, but he was at this final game. I should have yelled to Fitzie, but I desperately wanted to know what was being said in the meeting by the dugout. Boris seemed to be doing most of the talking, and I was about to wander down that way, when the meeting broke up. I saw Boris shake both the councilman's and chief's hands, and then the outfielder headed back for the playing field. It was almost as if something had been decided upon. I had to get Fitzie and I yelled out to the manager. He looked over and I shouted that Carmody wanted to see him in the office. He cussed and handed the bat over to one of his players to continue infield practice. He started for the office, and I decided to follow and see if I might be able to hear what Mr. Carmody wanted to tell the Owl's manager.

On his way through the outer office, Fitz picked up an old

159

tomato can. Will kept the can there so Fitzie could spit tobacco juice in the can rather than on the floor. Will didn't like ball players spitting on his floor, and since he didn't have a spittoon in the office, Fitzie carried the can.

Mr. Carmody greeted the manager. "Fitz, great to see you. How are things going?"

"Fair. We won the pennant."

"And we're all mighty proud of you. You're the only pennant winner in our farm system this year. Takes a little heat off me." Mr. Carmody was chuckling like it was a joke, but Fitzie didn't have much of a sense of humor.

"If you had some ball players, you'd win more pennants."

"Same old Fitz. One reason I wanted to talk to you was to get your feelings for next season. Given it any thought?"

"Same as always. I'd like a chance with a AAA club or at least a AA club."

"Yes, I'd thought you'd say that, but we've been thinking in terms of something else. You've been managing for over twenty years, and we'd like to spread your experience around. Frankly, I've been talking with the ownership, and we think you're being wasted on a Class B team. You've got too much knowledge to restrict it to just one club. We haven't really created a position yet, but I'm thinking of establishing some sort of roving position. That way you can go around and supervise all our minor league clubs, help out all the players, and just put your knowledge to better use."

"Hell, Carmody, I'm a manager. I can't spend one or two days with a player and make anything out of him. I need a season."

"You underestimate yourself, Fitz. Besides, I'll be honest. The club president feels we haven't been sending enough talent to the big leagues. He wants to change some of the managers in the minor league system. He knows the job you've done, and you're one of the few he wants to keep."

"Jesus Christ, Carmody. If he wasn't so tight with the purse strings and if he spent more money on players, he'd have some talent. You don't need to change managers. You need to get some ball players."

The two talked a little while longer. I really couldn't understand Fitzie's feelings. I didn't want to see him leave as manager of the Owl's, but it sure sounded impressive, him going around to all the minor league clubs and telling them what to do. But Fitzie kept saying things like they were "kicking him upstairs," and he repeated that he didn't like it. But Mr. Carmody kept talking real smooth, and you could tell the decision had already been made. Fitzie wasn't going to be a manager anymore. And I guess for someone who had been doing that most of his life, it bothered him. But I knew he would learn to live with it.

It was about time for the game to start, and Fitzie had to be on the field. He was about to leave when he asked Mr. Carmody one last question.

"If I'm not going to be in Centerville next year, who's gonna be the manager of the Owls?"

"That's the main reason I'm here, Fitz. There's not going to be a team in Centerville next year. Can you ask Will and the councilman to come in here?"

When I was a kid, I used to have this problem that people would say something to me and think I didn't hear. They would always be repeating stuff to me, when actually I'd heard every word. I would hear, but it would make no impression. Fitzie walked through the outer office and looked at me kind of funny, because he knew I could hear what was going on inside. But I just looked at him normal, because to be honest, it was like when I was younger. I had heard every word Mr. Carmody said, but it didn't register. He had said there wasn't going to be a team in Centerville next year, but it had nothing to do with me.

And so I just sat there, not thinking about much of anything. Then whatever was keeping it from my brain went down, and all of a sudden I knew what Mr. Carmody had said. There wasn't going to be a team in Centerville. There weren't going to be anymore Owls. It couldn't be. It had to be wrong. I had to do something. If I could keep Will from coming in the office, maybe Mr. Carmody would forget to tell him, and it might slip his mind that he was going to move the team. But my feet wouldn't move, and I couldn't get up from my desk. I saw Will and the councilman coming toward the office, and I knew I had to stop them. But I couldn't and Will smiled at me as he went through the front office into the main office. How could he smile? If I could have stopped him, he wouldn't have smiled, he wouldn't have walked into the office. But he was in now, and it was going to happen. The worst was going to happen.

I didn't want to stay now. I didn't want to hear anything. Once more I tried to get up from the desk, but again my feet didn't move. And I had to sit and listen as Mr. Carmody told them the Owls were going to move.

"Will, Councilman, please have a seat." The metal chairs scraped, and Mr. Carmody continued talking. Why couldn't he shut up? "Gentlemen, right now I'm going to have to do one of the hardest things I've ever done in baseball. I wish I didn't have to tell you this, but I'll be direct. We're not going to put a ball club in Centerville next year."

He had done it. He had told Will. For a while, it might have been forever, nobody said anything. Then I heard Will's voice. "The racial problem?"

"Yes, Will, it boils down to that. When I told you in June that we would stick by you, I firmly believed that. Even after the riot, I saw no reason we couldn't keep a club here. But in the past couple of weeks, there has been some serious thinking and reevaluation on this at the major league level. In the final week, Mr. Fleer, our owner, made the decision. He is still getting considerable pressure from national Negro organizations. But he does not want to impose on local custom here. For that reason he has instructed me to move our Class B club to the Three I League for next season."

The Three I League! How could anybody in Illinois or Iowa or Indiana or wherever care anything about the Centerville Owls. What difference did it make to them? People in Centerville cared about the Owls. It didn't make sense. How could the Owls play in Peoria or Keokuk or Terre Haute? It wasn't right.

The talking continued, but Will wasn't saying anything. It was

162

Councilman Waller. Maybe he could save the Owls. "Mr. Carmody, I realize the major league club doesn't want to make a decision concerning segregation here, but if it would make a difference I'm sure I could get the city council to agree to integrated seating at the park if you could keep the Owls here."

"I appreciate what you're saying, Councilman, but I'm afraid Mr. Fleer has made up his mind."

"But Centerville has been good for you. I simply can't believe that with one bad year you will desert us. I think I could get enough pledges from major industries in town to offset any losses you might have had this year. You know next year will be better."

"Councilman, anything I say might give you false hope. The decision is final and there is nothing you can do. I can only say that your one hope might be to persuade another major league club to come in here with a working agreement."

"Mr. Carmody. Let's be realistic. If you move out and with the publicity we've gotten this year, no other major league club would touch this town with a ten-foot pole. If you say the decision is final, I can only accept your word. But I hope you realize what this is doing. We've got fans who have been coming out here for twenty-five years and longer, and now you're taking something out of their lives. All year long you've given us assurances that everything is OK, that we just need to sit things out, and now on the last day you tell us you're moving out and there is nothing we can do."

"Mr. Waller, I feel as badly as you. I like Centerville, and the club has been a good one for us. But when a decision is made above me, all I can do is follow orders. That's why I wanted to come and personally tell you, because this is a big shock for me also."

The men talked. It seemed like I had been tied to my chair all night. I knew that Maggie had come in long ago for her tickets, that the game had started, that everything was happening like it always happened when Centerville had a game. Only this was the last time.

163

The conversation ended. Mr. Carmody asked Will not to say anything to the press yet. He wanted the major league club's public relations department to write up a release in a few days. And then the three men walked out. Will was the last, and I was surprised how calm he looked. When he went by me, he put his fingers to his lips. "Don't say anything, Tom," and he left. I sat at my desk, not knowing what to think or feel.

The game was going on, but I didn't care. I could look out to the front gate from the office, but nobody was coming in. The pickets did not come anymore, and Mr. Johnson was just standing, waiting for the fans that would never come. Will wandered in and out of the office a couple of times, but I didn't look at him. He was trying to act like it was a normal game. He did things he always did during a game, except how could he mean it? Who cared if the rest rooms had toilet paper or the hot dogs were cooked? We would lose all our fans anyway.

In a while Maggie came in. Lately she had been coming in when things were slow out front, and Mr. Johnson would yell if a fan came. And she had this bouncy smile and looked all happy. She didn't know. But she stopped when she came into the office and looked at me. I was trying to act normal, for Will had said I shouldn't tell anybody. And Maggie didn't come in any further, but she turned around and went out.

I was still sitting when she came in a few minutes later, and she gave me another smile. Only this time it was a sad smile. She came up and hugged me, and I guess it's the first time I hugged somebody back other than my mother that I can remember. The whole time Maggie didn't say anything, and I guess by then I was crying, but Maggie let me hug. Then she left and went back to her ticket booth, because a final fan was coming in.

I should have stayed in the office until it was time to check Maggie in, but it was the only time in the four years I'd been working at the park that I didn't check the ticket seller in. I didn't care. It didn't matter, for who really cared how many people were there to see the Centerville Owls? It didn't matter if the Owls made any money.

I wandered out of the office, and Donald came up. He said something, and he knew the Owls were moving. I asked him how he knew, and he said Councilman Waller had been telling everyone and was really angry about it. I looked over at Mr. Johnson, and he knew. He came up and gave me a pat on the back. I saw Mr. Carmody walk by, and he went to the concession stand to order a hot dog. Normally, the people in the concession were just as friendly as they could be to Mr. Carmody. But nobody at the stand was saying anything to him. They knew it.

And then I heard these little chugging steps coming from behind, and I looked and saw Miss Elmira, broom in hand, heading for Mr. Carmody. She was going to tell him off, and I had to stop her. As she passed I grabbed her arm. It was the first time I'd ever grabbed Miss Elmira, but I couldn't see her telling off Mr. Carmody.

Elmira stopped, and it wasn't a friendly expression she gave me as she looked me in the eyes. "Why you grab me, boy?"

"Elmira, where are you going?"

"It's not your business, boy, but I'm going to give that man a piece of my mind."

"You can't Elmira. It's not his fault. He didn't make the decision. He's just carrying out orders."

"Orders. Humpphh! And where's them orders leave you, boy? What you gonna do now that you livin' with a man who just lost his job? You think you can still live with yo' uncle. And Mr. Will. What he gonna do with them orders? They gonna put bread on his table and in yo' mouth? He jes' lost his job, and you tellin' me not to give him a piece of my mind. And him and Miss Maggie. You think yo' uncle gonna marry that girl if he can't support her? Where's that leave her? Where's his orders leave all them people who be comin' out to the games fo' years now ain't got nothing to do."

I didn't know what to say, but whatever I said wouldn't have mattered to Miss Elmira, because she was all worked up. "No, boy, you get yo' hand off me, 'cause I got to say somethin' to that

165

man. Mr. Will's a nice man, but that's his problem. He's jes' too nice sometime, and he won't say what he should. And boy, you ain't much better. There's time for bein' nice and time for not bein' nice, and this is a not bein' nice time." I dropped my hand, and Miss Elmira strode up to Mr. Carmody. He started to say something to her, but he didn't get a chance because she was shaking her broom in his face. But I guess whatever she had wanted to say just didn't come out, because all she muttered was, "It's a shame, a cryin' shame," and she turned around and marched off.

I stood there for a while, not sure of what I should do, and then I started for the stands. I would watch the game and concentrate on the men running after the ball and think of nothing else. Donald was behind me as I walked out to the field. I turned to him.

"Where you sitting?"

"I'm not. I'm bat boy again."

"Where's Millard?"

"He's here, but his father asked me last inning to take over. I think he wanted to tell Millard about the team moving."

I looked over to the councilman's seat and saw the two sitting there. Millard looked disturbed as the councilman talked, and I wondered if he understood.

Donald was about to go on the field to his bats when I stopped him. I had glanced over to the third base coach's box, and Hugh McDowell, the Owls' first baseman, was there. Where was Fitzie? I asked Donald.

"Aw, you really missed it, Tom. Right before the game, Fitzie came out and yelled up to the stands that he was giving the fans a special treat, Hugh McDowell running the club for the final game. Fitzie bowed to the stands and everything, and since then McDowell's been managing the club. Can you believe that? McDowell don't have shit for brains."

Everything was messed up. It must have been Fitzie's idea of a joke, because McDowell sure didn't have good sense. Donald was arranging bats, and I started out to the bleachers. There were only about 250 people in the stands, and most of them were sitting in the grandstand. No one was making any noise, but people aren't supposed to make noise at funerals. This was the end of the Owls.

I looked out to the scoreboard to see the score, but that was messed up too. No numbers had been put up, and it looked like Monty wasn't out there. He wasn't because when I reached the end of the bleachers I saw him sitting by himself. I went over and sat next to him.

"Why aren't you out on the scoreboard?"

"Why should I?"

"It's your job."

"Who cares?"

"Who's gonna pull up the owl?"

"I don't give a damn about that stupid bird."

Monty had heard about the team, and he refused to answer any more of my questions. He just sat, looking straight ahead. So I sat with him, not saying anything, watching a game whose score I didn't know.

I had been there a few minutes when I heard a voice calling my name. It was coming from the bullpen, and I stood up to see who was calling me. It was Fitzie. Piedmont was sitting with him, and they were out there alone, watching the game.

Fitzie kept calling me, and I went down to see what he wanted. He was talking like he had been drinking. "Tom, me and Piedmont here are getting a bit thirsty, and we run out of beer. How about hustling down to the concession stand and bringing us back a few cool ones."

I looked at Fitzie's feet and saw a pile of empty cans. "What-'cha doing out here, Fitzie?"

"Tom, you ain't much at shinin' shoes, but you got a little sense, and you may have noticed that I'm about the best manager in organized baseball. However, Carmody and some of his fat-assed friends aren't smart enough to know that, and they're putting me out to pasture. So I'm quittin' a day early and givin' them just what they deserve. I'm puttin' the dumbest human

167

being I know in charge tonight, that red-headed bastard you see down at third base. I'm letting him run the team. That's what they want, so I'll give it to them. Also, this lets me drink beer with my friend, Piedmont, here. So now get your ass in gear and go get us some beer."

Fitzie was as drunk as I'd ever seen him, and Piedmont wasn't much better off. I headed for the concession stand. Stewart gave me a case for them, which seemed like more than they needed, but Stewart said he had to get rid of it, and nobody he'd rather give it to than Fitzie. When I got back, Piedmont and Fitzie acted like I'd been gone forever, but they were really happy I had a case with me. I decided not to sit in the bleachers, and I stayed in the bullpen. Fitzie didn't throw me out as I sat in the grass behind their bench. In a little while Monty came down and sat beside me in the grass, but he still wasn't talking.

We found out the score in the bottom of the fifth inning when Boris came out and sat in the grass with Monty and me. The Owls were leading 4 to 0. Boris kept sitting there when the team wasn't in the field. During this whole time Fitzie was carrying on a running conversation with Piedmont. Piedmont's chief contribution to the conversation seemed to be saying "Tha's right," as Fitzie talked about a number of subjects, the main theme concerning the stupidity of the major league club.

"Now, Piedmont, you take that boy sitting over there. He's got a fine uncle, a fine man. And do you know what the big league club's doin' to that man? Why, they're taking away his ball club and leavin' him without a job. Piedmont, they're leaving you without a team. They're takin' it away from Centerville, a fine little baseball town. And Piedmont, you know who I feel worse about than anybody else is that kid sittin' beside Tom. You know, he put the eyes in the owl out there. Nothin' I liked better than to see him jump off that scoreboard and pull his owl up. And now, I don't guess he'll ever pull it up again.

"Piedmont, you see my rightfielder. Fine baseball veteran. They love him in Centerville, and he loves the town. But do you think they love him some place in Iowa? Why they don't know him. You think he'll have a job next year? Yes sir, that Carmody really came in and did a job tonight."

Fitzie kept on talking. The Owls were playing the Wilson Tobs, and Wilson started scoring some runs. Fitzie forgot about talking how stupid the big league club was and started talking about Hugh McDowell. He wasn't saying good things. Hughie was giving signs right and left, and the way he was acting you might have thought it was the seventh game of the World Series. Except you knew whatever he was doing was dumb, and it was getting Fitzie mad.

The ball park had been silent for six innings. Nobody had cheered or booed or anything, but now Fitzie, drunk, was yelling at McDowell at the top of his lungs. Everybody in the stands was looking out, and I could see Will sitting with Maggie and the councilman and Millard staring out. Fitzie kept on yelling, and when the Tobs scored another run, Fitzie screamed again. "You dumb, red-headed bastard. Get somebody down here to warm up." Finally, McDowell sent a pitcher to the bullpen to get warm.

Fitzie and Piedmont were still putting away the beer, but in the seventh inning Wilson started to score again. Fitzie was getting red in the face. "You put an idiot in to manage, and sure enough, he manages like an idiot." Finally, when Wilson scored two runs to go ahead 5 to 4, it was more than he could take. He opened a fresh can of beer, wobbled up off the bench, and yelled so the entire ball park could hear. "I'm taking over, McDowell," and he started weaving across the outfield grass to the infield.

I don't know who started it, and when I first heard it, I thought the sound was really out of place, like somebody whistling in church. High in the grandstand someone started clapping as Fitzie staggered across the grass to the pitcher's mound. It was only one person at first, but then another person picked it up, and down in the box seats somebody whistled, and it just kept rising and rising as Fitzie got to the mound. I saw everybody in the stands get up to their feet, and they were yelling and cheering

169

and really going wild. It was as if someone had just hit a grand-slam home run in the bottom of the ninth inning. I don't ever remember so much noise at the park, and for 250 people, it must have been the most noise ever made. And the only thing that had happened was Fitzie, drunk as a skunk, had decided he was going back to manage. As he waited for a new pitcher to come, he bowed to the fans, and they yelled even louder.

I got to thinking as I sat out in the grass with Monty that the fans weren't cheering Fitzie as much as they were cheering all the good things about the Centerville Owls. The 250 people who had stayed with the Owls had been coming out to the games for years, and I think when Fitzie came in it reminded them that the games were supposed to be fun. Even if this was the last one, they were going to make the last couple of innings good. And they kept on cheering.

In the bottom of the seventh inning, Fitzie signaled to the bull-pen again. I couldn't understand it. A pitcher wasn't warming up, and the only people out there were me and Monty and Pied-mont. Then I realized he was pointing at Piedmont who had fallen asleep. I punched the groundskeeper, and he woke up. It was apparent that Fitzie wanted Piedmont to come to the dugout and bring the beer. Piedmont started with the beer under one arm, and he wasn't going so straight when Fitzie met him halfway to the infield. The two of them opened some more beer even before they reached the dugout, and the crowd loved it. It looked like the umpires wanted to say something, because drinking on the field was not tolerated in the Carolina League, but Fitzie waved them away. The umpires didn't say anything else, and they must have felt there wasn't much point in getting in an argument with a half-drunk manager on the final day of the season.

In the eighth inning everything happened. The Owls were still behind 5 to 4, but when they came to bat in the bottom of that inning the fans kept up their cheering because they really wanted the team to win. The first two batters made outs. Then there was a single and a double, and the Owls had runners on second and third with Boris coming to bat. He tipped his hat to the crowd and rubbed his hands with the resin bag, and he was really putting on a little show before he came to bat. But I know he wanted to get a hit as much as everyone in the stands wanted one, and he really concentrated as he stared out at the pitcher.

The first two pitches were balls, and he fouled off the next two. Then, almost like it was in a movie, he hit a high drive to deep center field. The Wilson outfielder kept running back. He still was running when he reached the fence and could go no further as the ball sailed over the wall. For a moment the place was silent and then everybody let out a yell and I was on my feet jumping up and down and Monty was pounding me on the back.

It was after Boris crossed home plate that things happened that I never was quite clear on. I saw Boris go into the dugout and talk to Fitzie and then with the crowd still cheering he came out and waved his hand. He went back to the dugout and shook his teammates' hands, and then he started running toward Monty and me in the bullpen. As he neared us, he yelled to Monty. "Hey, I thought that owl of yours was supposed to go up after a home run," and Monty leapt to his feet and started following Boris across the center field grass.

The only other time I'd been on the field during a game was back in July, but I didn't hesitate. I was right behind Monty and Boris as we passed the Wilson outfielders and headed toward the scoreboard. We went through the door in the outfield fence, and Boris was climbing the back of the scoreboard. He had this big grin on his face, as wide as could be, and he was laughing. He grabbed hold of Monty's rope and let out a yell as he jumped off. And Monty's owl came up with horn honking and eyes flashing. Boris yelled up to us. "God, I've wanted to do that for a long time."

By then both of us were on the scoreboard, and Boris threw the rope up to Monty. This time Monty jumped off, and he was yelling and laughing. Again the owl came up. I looked back to the grandstand and the field, and the game had not started back up. All the Wilson players were staring out at the crazy people on

171

the scoreboard, and I could hear the fans yelling in the grandstand. Out in front of the dugout it looked like Fitzie and Piedmont were doing some kind of drunken dance.

Boris yelled up to me as Monty threw me the rope. "Tommy, it's been great, but I've got to get going. If you ever need to know, talk to Mr. Waller." And I stood there with the rope waiting to jump as Boris started running again, this time behind the fence and around the stadium to his car. I knew it would be the last time I would see him.

It was my time to jump, to make the owl come up, and as I started to jump I saw another figure running across the outfield. It was Millard. I couldn't figure out why he was running, but I thought it might be because he wanted to see the owl up close. But as he came through the fence door, he didn't look over our way. He just kept running in his funny way, and he was running after Boris. Boris was almost out of sight, almost to his car, and it would have been impossible for Millard to catch up. But he kept running.

At first I didn't know what to think, but then I realized that Millard didn't understand everything, but he knew the Owls were going. When he saw Boris leaving, he must have thought he could catch him and stop the team from going. I jumped off the scoreboard, holding the owl's rope, and it came up for the third time. I quickly handed the rope to Monty and let him flash the eyes and blow the horn. Somebody had to stop Millard. I started running again, this time after Millard. I didn't really know how I was going to stop him, but when I caught up with him in the parking lot, I just tackled him. Boris's car was fading in the distance. Millard was much bigger than I was, and I had to really hold tight. I was lying on top, and he was crying and trying to yell after Boris.

Boris's car was gone, but I still stayed there on top of Millard, telling him everything was going to be all right. I knew everything probably wasn't going to be all right, but I had to stop him from crying. Most of the stuff was just adult talk when you don't say everything you mean, but Millard calmed down. And as we were lying there, I remembered that once before I had tackled Millard and held him down, trying to calm him, and that was the night my father died. But I pushed that out of my mind. I didn't want to remember it.

We were out in the parking lot a long time before Will and Maggie found us. Only then did I get off Millard, and the four of us walked back into the ball park. As we reached the field, I heard the owl's horn and saw it rising on the scoreboard. The teams were leaving the field. The Owls had won, and everything was over.

The old man is telling a story, but by now you have remembered much of it. It is the story of a murder by a son who killed his father with an iron pipe. But when he tried to drag the body, it was too heavy. He could not move it. The boy remembered someone he had seen earlier in the park, and he went and found a frightened retarded man who was running away. He had to chase the man and drag him down. But the retarded man was the boy's friend, and he calmed the man and talked him into helping.

Behind the fence the two of them fashioned a grave, and when they were done they came back to the park. The outfielder was there, for he had heard noises behind the fence. He saw the blood and dirt, and he took them to the clubhouse and cleaned the two. But neither could explain. The boy appeared to have forgotten everything, and the other could not make himself understood. *The outfielder sent the two home, but he became involved, for the job they did was crude, the grave inadequate, and that night he worked so no one would know. He covered the grave with underbrush and wiped away all traces of blood.*

For a long while it appeared that the body would never be found. But then the fence fell down, and the federal authorities pushed for a solution. The local police were close to solving the crime, but they knew it would involve the boy, the retarded man, and the outfielder. They did not want a solution. And so the outfielder agreed that he would run, provide the decoy, and the boy was protected.

The old man finishes his story, and the blood is drained from you. You say nothing, but the old man understands. He gets up to leave and hands you an old scrap of paper. It is an address and he is not sure if it is good any longer. Then he leaves, and you sit and stare at an old baseball field.

S OME people cry at weddings. I always thought it was silly,
except I was crying at Will's. After all that had happened, I
thought Will and Maggie would never get married, expecially
with Will not having a team anymore and both of them having
left Centerville. But it was happening, and I felt a little foolish.
Here I would be fifteen in a month and my eyes were all moist. I
don't think too many people saw me because I stared straight
ahead. Other people were crying too.

It was supposed to be a small, simple ceremony with only a
few people invited, and I was surprised at the number of people
who showed up. Somehow the word got around and half the old
Centerville Owl fans were there.

My mother drove up with me. Will had asked me to be the
best man, and I was really proud when he did, particularly since
I wasn't living with him anymore and he didn't have to. After the
final night of the season, things didn't stop happening. A week or
so later my grandmother died, and what with Will being without
a job and my mother being by herself, I moved back east. It was
really a tough decision, and they left it up to me. I wanted to stay
with Will, but my mother needed someone now. Living with
Will was about the best thing that had ever happened to me, and
leaving Monty and Donald and school in the middle was rough,
but all things considered, it was best for all that I go east.

After the season was over, Will and Councilman Waller and
some others tried to get another big league club to put a farm
team in Centerville, but as the councilman predicted, no big
league club would come to Centerville. Will wanted to stay in
Centerville, and he started looking for jobs. He wanted one that
would pay enough for him to support Maggie if she would
marry him, but he ran into some problems. He looked and

looked, but nobody wanted him. The real reason involved the racial problems. Everybody liked Will, but he was so associated with all the problems at the park, it scared people around town who might have hired him.

It turned out that Mr. Roth of Roth's Fine Men's Clothiers was the one who helped Will out. Will didn't even ask Mr. Roth for his old job, because he knew it could hurt the clothing business if Mr. Roth hired him. Also, being a clerk didn't pay so much. But one day about a month after the season, Mr. Roth called up Will and asked him why he hadn't been down to see him. Roth's had a branch in Chapel Hill, and he asked Will if he'd like to be an assistant manager. Well, that's what caused Will and Maggie to finally get married. Maggie had been accepted at Carolina law school for January, and although she didn't have enough money, the two of them decided to go ahead and try it.

Here Will had been so conscious about having enough money to provide for Maggie, and now it looked to me like both of them were going to do a good job at starving. Maggie would go to school during the day and work part time at night. Will would be working six days a week at Roth's while also taking some night courses. I always thought two people got married so they could see each other more often, but it sure seemed like they'd worked things so they'd never see each other. I decided not to tell Will it was dumb, because I didn't think it would do any good.

You wouldn't have believed the wedding. I imagine most people would have guessed it, but the ceremony was held at the ball park. I think it was the last event ever held in the stadium, and Will got special permission from Councilman Waller to use it. When Will first told me he was using the ball park I thought he was kidding. Then the more I thought about it, the more perfect I thought it would be. They held the ceremony at home plate, and all the box seat chairs were moved out on the infield.

Will had asked Mr. Johnson to be his head usher, and he was dressed in a tuxedo fit to kill. Piedmont had really gone to special trouble arranging the chairs and fixing up the park, and he even cut the grass and lined the field as if it were a game. He was sort of standing off to the side in a new blue suit, and although I think

178

he was a little drunk, he was smiling and everybody was telling him the field looked as good as it had ever looked.

I'd have never guessed who Maggie asked to be her matron of honor, but it was Miss Elmira. She was holding this pretty bunch of flowers and was telling everybody where to stand. She told Piedmont how to arrange the chairs, and I might have known even at a time like this she would want to boss everybody around. When I got there, she told me if I was going to be a best man I'd better look right, and she started straightening my tie. Then she gave me a big hug like I was something special. I didn't mind and I think some of the tears started then.

It was a Saturday, and the wedding was supposed to start at 2 P.M. Usually it starts to get cold in North Carolina about that time of year, but that day was warm and sunny, almost like baseball season. Will and Maggie were all smiling and happy, and I don't think anything could have been better.

I arrived around 1 P.M., and we all received instructions from the minister on where to stand and what I was supposed to do with the ring and all that. The reason only a few people had been invited was Will hadn't wanted a big to-do, but around 1:30 people started wandering in. Piedmont and Mr. Johnson had set out only about twenty-five chairs, but they kept going back for more. By the time the wedding was about to start you might have thought there was a ball game going on.

Millard was there with the councilman, and he was dressed in a new suit. You really couldn't tell he was retarded the way he looked. He was home for the weekend from his special school in Raleigh, and when he saw me he grinned and came up and shook my hand. Funny, but I was glad to see him. I could tell he was all excited, and I guess this was the first wedding he'd ever been to. Both Will and Maggie came up and made like he was the one person they wanted to see at the wedding. Councilman Waller was beaming, but he also was looking a little sad, I thought, because this was probably the last time he could bring Millard to the ball park. But the councilman perked up when he saw all the people coming in, because some of them were voters, but also they were his friends.

I don't know how Fitzie had gotten there, but Will said he'd written him, and I guess Fitz had driven all the way from Mississippi. He had officially resigned from the major league club in September, but he said he thought he was going to be able to hook on with another big league organization. I hoped so. And he'd brought Will and Maggie a wedding present I couldn't believe. It was this new, shiny, brass spittoon. I don't know where he'd found it, or what he expected them to do with it, but he said he was coming to visit them, and they'd probably need it for his visit. Fitzie and Piedmont were drinking from a brown paper bag, even before the wedding started, but it was good to hear him tell everybody that his ulcer hadn't acted up since he quit the big league team.

Right before the ceremony this kid on a bicycle rode up, and he was from Western Union with a telegram. I took it over to Will, but he asked me to open it and read it to them. I'd never read a telegram before. WITH DEEPEST LOVE AND BEST WISHES FOR ALL THE HAPPINESS THE WORLD CAN GIVE YOU. BORIS SULLIVAN. Well, how Boris knew Maggie and Will were getting married nobody knew. Nobody had seen or heard of him since the last game, but the telegram was from somewhere in upstate New York. Maggie took the telegram from me, and her eyes started to mist up. Will was just smiling.

The ceremony was beautiful, or at least that's what my mother told me. I really don't remember a bit of it. I just stood there as the minister read his lines, and when I was supposed to give the ring I did. My mind wasn't really on the service, and I was looking out at the people. For all the trouble we'd had during those last months, all the publicity, Centerville Stadium was finally integrated. All the old colored fans had shown up, and everybody was sitting and mingling together.

Stewart had arranged the reception, and rather than champagne, he'd brought a keg of beer. There were hot dogs and popcorn, and everybody was having a grand time. People were hugging and kissing Maggie, and Will had this silly grin on his face. I tried to tell him to do something about it, but he just kept on grinning. Fitzie and Piedmont got drunk together and started

180

singing. Miss Elmira was serving punch to those who weren't having beer. Of course, Monty and Donald showed up, and I think they were filling their punch cups with beer. The reason I think that, was I was doing it myself.

It was just as Will and Maggie were getting ready to leave for Chapel Hill and Stewart was passing out popcorn to throw at them, that I saw Monty and Donald ask Stewart to hold up everything for a minute. It might have had something to do with them drinking the beer, but they started running across the outfield whooping and yelling, and then I knew what they were going to do. As everybody started throwing popcorn at Will and Maggie, Monty jumped off the scoreboard, and the owl came up for the last time with his eyes flashing and horn blowing. I don't guess that happens at most weddings, but I don't believe Will or Maggie could have asked for anything better to top off their wedding than a ten-foot metal owl sitting on top of a fence making all sorts of racket.

After Will and Maggie left I didn't stay much longer, because we had the long drive back east. In a way I was a little sad driving away, because I knew I might never see some of those people again. I guess my mother knew what I was thinking, because she started talking about friends and keeping them. She said just knowing someone was your friend was enough, even if you might never see them again. And so we talked and I felt a little better, because so many of the people at the wedding were my friends, and it was something I could always have. But then I got sleepy, because riding always made me a little sleepy and I'd drunk some beer. I didn't wake until we got home.

You are driving once more. You are leaving a town you left many years earlier. But you are not headed for your original destination. You have an old slip of paper, an old address. It is probably no longer any good, but you must make the effort. You must try to find someone who helped you those many years before, for you never knew it. You drive, hoping it is not too late to say thank you.